FREAKLING

LING

Lana Krumwiede

CANDLEWICK PRESS

Copyright © 2012 by Lana Krumwiede

First edition 2012

Library of Congress Cataloging-in-Publication Data is available.

Library of Congress Catalog Card Number pending

ISBN 978-0-7636-5937-0

12 13 14 15 16 17 BVG 10 9 8 7 6 5 4 3 2 1

Printed in Berryville, VA, U.S.A.

This book was typeset in Berkeley Oldstyle Medium.

Candlewick Press
99 Dover Street
Somerville, Massachusetts 02144

visit us at www.candlewick.com

To the people who make my story better:
Kip, Tim, Julie, Ben, and Callie

•   •   •

PART ONE

1 ALLIGATOR

Each new cycle must begin
With Alligator creeping in.
Unseen danger now surrounds you.
New awareness must be found to
Conquer fear from deep within.
Conquer fear from deep within.

— CALENDAR SONG

The first time Taemon's brother tried to kill him was the night Uncle Fierre came over with his unisphere.

Mam was cooking sweet tubers and onions for dinner that night. Taemon caught a whiff of the rich aroma as he walked into the kitchen. A purple onion floated above the pot. After shedding its papery outer layers, it diced itself perfectly and fell into the stew. A sweet tuber peeled itself as neat slices dropped into the pot, its ruddy skin landing in the garbage. Tiny silvery leaves of an herb separated from their stems and joined the mixture. On the opposite side of the kitchen, dough kneaded itself on the counter-top, folding and flattening, folding and flattening.

Taemon marveled at how easily his mother used psi. He'd seen her cook a million times and never thought much of it. Now that he was twelve years old, finally learning to do real work with psi, he understood how much skill it took to do several things at once. Mam might not always show it, but her psi was plenty powerful.

When Taemon was very young, he hadn't even realized there was such a thing as psi. After dinner, the dishes would float to the kitchen and hover over the garbage pail. There they paused while the mess and food bits flung themselves into the pail. Then the perfectly clean dishes would drift into their places in the cupboard. Other things were like that, too. Doors knew when to open, water flowed from the faucet when needed, quadriders drove people from place to place.

One day when he was about three years old, Taemon realized dishes didn't wash themselves. Someone was using psi to tell the dishes and the doors and the quad-riders what to do. You couldn't see it, you couldn't hear it, but when an object moved, someone nearby was doing it with psi. Da said even the Earth had her psi. She used it to fetch rain from the clouds and rouse the seeds in spring.

His mother's voice interrupted Taemon's thoughts. "Fierre will be here soon."

"Good," he said, although he wasn't sure of that. Uncle Fierre and Da clashed when it came to politics. And Uncle Fierre was spending the summer solstice holiday with them. Tomorrow they would all drive out to the coast. Taemon hoped Da would keep the arguing to a minimum.

Taemon sat down on a stool next to the countertop where the dough was dividing itself into little pasty blobs. Watching the dough form itself into balls around pinches of spicy pork filling, Taemon decided he could put up with a fair amount of arguing if it meant pork balls for dinner.

His belly rumbled. Using psi, he lifted an apple from the basket on the counter. It hovered in front of him. He pictured clearly in his mind a large chunk of apple separating itself and drifting into his mouth. He held the image in his head for a split second and reached out with his mind toward the apple. *Be it so!*

And it happened just as he had pictured. Taemon opened his mouth and let the fruit chunk float in. His jaw tightened with its tartness.

"Not such big bites," Mam said.

How did she know? She had her back turned, looking out the window. Probably watching for Uncle Fierre.

Taemon directed another bite, only a tad smaller, from the apple toward his mouth. Using psi wasn't that hard, once you got used to it. You had to be able to picture it exactly in your mind, which meant you had to have some knowledge of the thing you were doing. Breaking off a piece of apple was simple. Other things were more complicated, like driving a quadrider. His brother Yens was sixteen and had gotten his license just last month, though Mam and Da rarely let him use their quadrider. Not till he'd learned to be more cautious, Mam said.

A thunderous roar ripped into the quiet afternoon. Taemon lost his concentration and the next apple chunk plopped on the counter. The pork balls dropped to the counter too, but Mam had let them down gently. The noise came from down the street.

"What in the Great Green Earth?" Mam craned her neck to get a wider view from the window.

Taemon walked over to Mam to take a look. He saw a byrider speeding down the street. No, not a byrider. It was one of those new unispheres. Instead of two wheels, it had one big ball that pivoted and swiveled like the tip of an old-world ballpoint pen that Taemon had seen once at the museum. The rumble paused as the unisphere changed gears, then the throaty growl broke out again.

Could anything be more thoroughly cool?

Mam sighed. "They never should have made those things legal." She turned back to her pork balls, and they began dipping themselves into the boiling broth.

Taemon leaned forward and squinted. "It's Uncle Fierre."

Once again the pork balls were abandoned as Mam turned her attention to the approaching unisphere. She huffed. "What is Fierre doing with one of those monstrosities? He's forty-six years old, for Sky's sake."

Uncle Fierre, a unisphere, and pork balls. Tonight ought to be interesting.

Taemon leaned back in his chair and waited for dessert. He had already eaten two bowls of sweet tuber stew and nine pork balls. If he ate any more, he would burst before the nut cake was served. As usual, the adults were taking forever to eat. They were too busy talking.

"The Emerald team has a real shot at the gold cup this year," Yens said. "Did you see the match last week?"

"I saw Kantall sink a few lucky shots," Uncle Fierre said. "But they'll have to be more consistent. He's too easy to predict."

Yens was the school's star athlete, and Uncle Fierre took it upon himself to give his nephew a few psiball pointers, seeing as Da had no interest in sports. Da saw the game as a fine way to teach youngsters psionic skill but not a proper pursuit for grown men and women.

As the psiball discussion continued, Taemon watched Da carefully to see if he would rise to the bait. So far, his father seemed to be showing restraint.

"I'm pretty sure I'll be elected captain of the team this year," Yens boasted, "which will help my chances when the high priest decides to choose the True Son."

Uncle Fierre nodded. "Couldn't hurt."

"It's not for the high priest to decide who the True Son is!" Da slammed down his mug with psi. "The Heart of the Earth will decide."

Uncle Fierre frowned, lifted his napkin with psi, and

dabbed at the corners of his mouth. "That's not what the priests are saying. They're working on selecting the True Son. It could very well be someone from our own family." Uncle Fierre fixed his gaze squarely on Yens.

Yens beamed.

Taemon used psi to make spiral patterns in the grease spots left on his plate. Could Uncle Fierre be right? Would the high priest choose Yens? After all, Mam was a descendant of the prophet Nathan, and that's the line the True Son was supposed to come from. And Yens's birth sign was Knife, which was the only other thing the scriptures specified.

"Have another pork ball, Fierre, and stop putting foolishness into Yens's head," Mam said softly. "We've waited two centuries for the True Son, and we may well wait two more."

"We'll know soon enough. They're going to announce the date of the next cycle sometime in the coming weeks." Uncle Fierre used psi to float three more pork balls to his plate. Taemon sat back in his chair. At this rate, he might be eating nut cake for tomorrow's breakfast.

"The Heart of the Earth will choose," Da said. "Not you, not I, and not the high priest."

"It's the same thing," Uncle Fierre said. "The high priest speaks for the Heart of the Earth."

Da frowned. "In theory."

"Stop right there." Uncle Fierre held his hand up, palm outward. "I sincerely hope you're not voicing these opinions in public, Wiljamen." He locked eyes with Da, a prickly silence growing between them.

Taemon lowered his head and stealthily glanced from face to face. Mam fidgeted with the edge of the tablecloth.

Yens plunged into the argument again. "He's right, Da. You of all people should accept the priests' authority."

Taemon watched Da press his mouth into a line and take a deep breath. Da was a religion teacher, the one who imparted the teachings of the prophet Nathan to school-children. He and Yens often argued about the appropriate uses of psi. Da clung to the traditional rules that safe-guarded the use of psi, while Yens followed the popular ideas that pushed its limits. They were always at odds, Yens and Da; even their birth signs were opposite. Yens, the Knife, causing division and strife. Da, on the other hand, was Stone, firm and unyielding. No wonder the sparks flew between them like flint and steel. Now would be a good time for Mam to bring in that nut cake.

"What do you think, Taemon?" Da asked. "Do the priests follow the Heart of the Earth?"

Taemon froze. This was a new element in the argument. Did Da seriously expect him to answer? How was he supposed to know why the priests did what they did? He should stay out of this. Say something neutral that wouldn't make anyone mad. He coughed to stall for time.

Da sighed and continued without Taemon's answer. "Psi is a gift from the Heart of the Earth," he said, measuring his words with exaggerated patience. "A person unites with the Earth's spirit, and if his heart is pure, his will becomes one with the will of the Earth. Psi was meant to accomplish that which is good for humankind. Not selfish gain. Not idle amusement. If Elder Naseph is planning on choosing the True Son himself and dictating the start of the New Cycle, then I'm telling you he is acting outside his authority."

Uncle Fierre gasped. "You go too far, Wiljamen! That's blasphemy. What possible reason could the high priest have for going against the will of the Earth?"

Taemon was just as curious as Uncle Fierre to know the answer to that question. But before Da could respond, Mam, ever the peacemaker, spoke up.

"Why don't you boys have a look at the unisphere?" she said. "I'll call you when it's time for dessert. Is that all right, Fierre?"

"Sure," Uncle Fierre said, obviously grateful for the distraction. "You can even sit on it if you like."

"Is it safe?" Mam asked.

He nodded. "It's stable enough with the emergency brake in place."

Yens was instantly out of his seat, heading for the back door, which was already opening with the help of psi. Taemon followed.

Uncle Fierre called out after them: "But you don't have permission to start it."

Yens reached the unisphere first and planted himself on the seat. "Ever seen one of these up close?" he asked.

Taemon shook his head.

"I have." Yens leaned forward and squeezed the hand grips. "Andon's brother has one. He showed us how it works."

Taemon took a moment to admire the machine.

The tire, if it was even called a tire, was a big black rubber ball with a tread that was patterned after alligator skin.

The tire-ball had a cap on top, like an upside-down bowl that covered more than half the ball. The sun gleamed off the shiny chrome of the cap, except for where an alligator symbol was etched in black on the sides. The fierce emblem made the unisphere look dangerous even when it sat in the driveway. On top of the chrome cap was a black leather seat that had a slight curve to it.

But where was the engine?

Even a unisphere had to have an engine of some kind. You couldn't just roll the ball forward. It wouldn't go very fast, not unless you exerted a lot of psi. And you'd get tired in a minute or two, just like with running. Psi engines didn't need fuel like in the old days, but there had to be gears and cams and springs to transfer the energy so a person didn't have to exert himself so much. There had to be an engine somewhere on this thing.

Taemon frowned. Usually he could figure out the general idea behind a machine, even if he didn't know enough details to operate it. But this unisphere had him stumped.

Of course, that was the whole point of psi. You had to know how something worked. You had to picture in your mind exactly what the machine looked like, parts and all, and then tell those parts what to do. If you didn't know clearly and precisely how something was to be done, you couldn't use psi to do it.

The more he stared at the unisphere, the more Taemon had to know how it worked. He was tempted to do something he hadn't done since he was a little kid. He was tempted to let his mind wander.

When Taemon first learned to use psi, he used to send out a small tendril of his mind to explore the world, like an ant scouting things out. It wasn't quite the same as using psi, because it could only explore, not move or change anything. But Da had made it clear that mind wandering was bad. Never to be done, never to be spoken of. He had been strict about it, so much so that Taemon had never told anyone else about it, not even Mam or Yens. Now that Taemon was older, he had figured out why. It was different. And different was suspicious. And suspicious was dangerous.

So Taemon stood there staring at the unisphere, wishing he knew where the engine was and how the crazy thing worked. If he used his mind wandering, he could figure it out. As long as he never acted on that knowledge, no one would ever know.

And that was the whole point, right? No one should ever know.

Taemon closed his eyes and let his awareness drift across the hard, rough concrete that was the driveway. Along the ridges and patterns of the unisphere's ball tire. Skimming the smooth surface of the chrome. He let his mind wander under the seat, where Yens sat tall and proud, as though he owned the thing. No engine there. Just thick padding and springs for shock absorption. He sent his mind lower, exploring the underside of the chrome cap. He could see it all in his head. Nothing there. He went deeper, inside the ball itself.

So there you are, thought Taemon.

Such a clever engine it was, too! Springs coiled tightly so the driver could release the energy as fast or slowly as needed. Tread on the inside of the tire as well, which fit perfectly with the cam. Only this was more complicated because—

"Hoy, freakling," Yens said sharply. "You getting on or not?"

Taemon nodded and scrambled up behind Yens. The seat was made for one, but they were both skinny and the inward curve of the seat kept them pressed together.

"Bet I could drive this thing," Yens said.

"We don't have permission."

That was the great safeguard of psi. You couldn't do anything that was outside of your authority. If you tried it, the internal conflict inside you blocked psi. So it was pretty much impossible to use psi to do anything that went against your conscience even in the slightest.

"So?" Yens said.

A bad feeling was growing in the pit of Taemon's stomach. What was Yens planning to do?

"He said we didn't have permission to start it. He didn't say we couldn't release the emergency brake." Yens's voice was quiet and frightening.

"Why?" Taemon asked. "So we can roll down the driveway and fall over? That would just be stupid."

Instantly Taemon regretted the last part of that comment. He had probably just multiplied Yens's determination to do whatever insane thing he had in mind.

"I'm getting off," Taemon said. He tried to swing his leg over the seat, but Yens leaned back, pinning Taemon in place.

"Not yet," Yens said. He reached down with his left

hand and released the brake. Immediately they began to roll backward.

Taemon gasped. He pulled his legs up as high as he could. When they fell over, he'd prefer not to get crushed between the ball and the ground.

But they didn't fall over. They kept rolling. Yens must have been using psi to balance the seat above the ball.

Now they were past the driveway and into the street. Yens couldn't start the engine without permission. So they were just going to roll the whole time? Taemon began to relax. Their street didn't have much of a slope. They wouldn't get far.

"Now comes the fun part," Yens said.

The bad feeling in Taemon's stomach was back in an instant. A quadrider was coming toward them on the street, and Yens seemed to be steering toward it.

"Uh, Yens?" Taemon tried not to sound terrified. "Shouldn't we try to avoid the quadrider?" His voice cracked.

Yens laughed and stayed his course. "That's the ticket, Tae. Put your life on the line, and you can do anything you want with psi."

Life on the line? Holy Mother Mountain!

The quadrider honked frantically. There was no room for it to pass—not with the unisphere in the middle of the street.

"Yens!" Taemon cried.

Just then, Taemon felt the engine starting up underneath him. The unisphere jerked and whined. Suddenly Taemon realized what Yens had done. In urgent danger, the survival instinct sometimes became stronger than a person's conscience and psi could be used if the person kept a calm head.

Sometimes.

They picked up speed. The unisphere sputtered. Lurched. Wobbled. This is exactly why psi was such a tricky thing. Authority, knowledge, state of mind—all of these played against each other and you could mess things up if you didn't stick to what you absolutely knew you could do.

Yens was losing control.

The quadrider honked again, mere feet away from them.

Before Taemon knew what was happening, Yens launched himself from the unisphere and tumbled into the grass at the side of the road.

Taemon wobbled, but even as he did so, he could feel his psi taking over. Once he made the decision to stay on the seat, all anxiety left him. His mind was clear and calm.

He knew how to drive the unisphere.

In one complete image, he pictured it in his head. The spring releasing the stored energy. The gears moving forward in a burst of speed. The steering mechanism pulling hard to the left. The seat staying balanced above the ball. It all came to his mind precisely and instantly. He gathered his psi and directed it toward the unisphere. *Be it so!*

Taemon hung on as he rocketed forward off the road and onto the grass, missing the quadrider by inches. He righted his course, then bounced back onto the road, flinging dry pine needles behind him.

He exhaled slowly. It wouldn't do to crash now. He had to stay calm a little longer.

He drove around the block and willed himself to be at peace.

The wind had smeared purple and gray across the twilit sky.

A squirrel bounded across the road.

The crickets began their song of darkness.

And Taemon parked Uncle Fierre's unisphere in the driveway.

Once he put the emergency brake on and withdrew his psi, the fear came back in a rush. He had come within a breath of dying. He started shaking.

Taemon stumbled off the seat. His legs felt too weak to stand. But before he could steady himself, Yens yanked him sideways and shoved him up against the splintery rough wood of their fence. He wedged his forearm across Taemon's neck. Even stronger than the pain and fear was the humiliation of being manhandled. Yens was attacking Taemon, which meant he had to do it with his hands. To use psi against another person, you had to be defending, assisting, or showing affection. And Yens was doing none of these.

"How did you drive it? You said you'd never seen one before."

"I had to do something." Taemon choked out the words. "You almost got us killed!"

Tiny splinters dug into his scalp as Yens pushed harder, forcing Taemon's chin up and his head back.

"Tell me what you did just now," Yens said, a terrible fierceness in his voice. "You shouldn't be able to do that."

His brother let the pressure off long enough for Taemon to gasp out a few words. "I can't. I don't even know what I did."

"Taemon! Yens!" Mam called from the house. "Time for nut cake!"

Yens slammed him against the fence again. "You'll tell me. I'll make sure of it." He let go and walked away.

Taemon sucked in short breaths and forced his tears back. He never should have allowed his mind to wander. It was bad, like Da said. What about what Yens had done? Placing yourself in danger so you can act outside authority?

Cha. That was bad, too.

2 MONKEY

Now as Alligator dies,

Monkey's day is on the rise.

Mischief, tricks, and goings-on

Can have a way of going wrong.

Playful Monkey loves surprises.

Playful Monkey loves surprises.

— CALENDAR SONG

Taemon sat in the backseat of the quadrider, with the luggage under his feet. Da was driving, Mam sat next to him, Yens and Uncle Fierre sat in the middle seats, and Taemon sat facing the back. It was just as well. Last night's argument had picked up again, and he could steer clear of the bickering by sitting all the way back. At the moment, Yens was badgering Da.

"One of these days, you're going to have to admit that the old ways don't matter anymore."

"Strength comes in many forms," Da said. "Psi is only one of them."

Yens snorted.

Taemon turned back to the view from the rear window, letting the others argue to their hearts' content. They drove east toward the shore, passing the farmland that fed the city. In the backseat Taemon faced west, watching the city wall grow smaller in the distance and admiring the mountains that rose behind Deliverance. At their base they were green and lush with the early summer rain. Higher, the peaks were craggy, a row of spikes that protected the city from the rest of the world.

It had been Taemon's own ancestor, the prophet Nathan, who had yanked those mountains out of flat ground. Talk about some powerful psi. Nathan was the one who discovered it. Only Da wouldn't use the word *discovered*. Da said that the Heart of the Earth granted psi to the prophet Nathan because he was so righteous that he would never use it to hurt anyone or do anything selfish. Either way you look at it, Nathan was the first one to have the power to visualize something and make it so.

It had been over two hundred years since Nathan had fled from the Republik with his family and friends during the Great War. You'd think a person with psi would be revered, but the opposite was true. People had feared Nathan, despised him. The Republikite army had wanted to use him as a weapon in the Great War, but Nathan refused. He and his followers moved to a wilderness area by the coast and built the city of Deliverance. Nathan passed psi on to his children and his followers' children, charging them to use it for good. Before long, Deliverance became a city of psi wielders. They tried to keep to themselves, but the Republik still harassed them. So Nathan used his psi to make the very mountains Taemon was staring at right now, the mountains that kept them separate from the rest of the world. The world finally got the idea and left them alone. Even now, there was no contact at all with the psiless cities of the Republik and the powerless people that lived on the other side of those mountains.

Taemon wondered how people lived without psi. Their lives must be so primitive. Did they even have running water? How would you turn it off without psi? It would have to have a lever of some kind that would move up and down to control the flow. Or maybe something like a screw would work better. But how would you turn a screw without psi?

Thinking up crazy machines and gadgets was Taemon's favorite way to daydream. Soon his brain had moved from psiless faucets to Uncle Fierre's unisphere. He saw its engine so clearly in his mind. As images swam through his head, his fingers twitched with anticipation; he longed to draw the unisphere.

He could do it. Da had given a journal to each of his boys as a way to encourage them to practice reading and writing. Yens had thrown his away, but Taemon had been filling his pages with sketches, bits of ideas, and questions about how things worked. His journal was tucked inside his suitcase, which was underneath his feet.

But he shouldn't. If anyone saw his drawing of the unisphere, he'd be hard-pressed to explain how he'd seen the engine. Not only that, but reading and writing were old-fashioned and thoroughly uncool. Most people didn't even know how to read anymore, and only those who had to keep records knew how to write—the clerks in the guilds, the priests in the churches. Prestige and privilege went to people who could wield psi with skill and talent.

And who would be foolish enough to write down all that hard-earned knowledge in a book where anyone could steal it? Might as well give away all your money.

But the urge had taken hold of Taemon, and it wouldn't leave until he'd drawn what was speeding through his mind.

He set to work using psi to rearrange the luggage, stacking it on the seat as a barricade between himself and the rest of the family. He padded a corner with the beach blankets Mam had packed, a space just big enough to curl up in with his journal. With his back to the family and the luggage piled up between them, no one would notice that he was writing.

Now to get his journal. He located his suitcase and used psi to unzip the outside pocket of the bag and imagined the journal easing out of the pocket and into his hands. *Be it so!*

Nothing happened.

Hmm. Maybe he hadn't put it in the pocket. He opened the main compartment with psi and prepared to rummage by hand through the swimming gear, underwear, and T-shirts.

But as soon as the bag was opened, Taemon realized his

mistake: this was Yens's suitcase, not his own. The bags were identical, and Taemon had mixed them up when he'd rearranged the luggage.

Something caught his eye. The tan corner of a book poking out from underneath a shirt. Taemon's heart raced. What was his journal doing in Yens's suitcase? Had Yens stolen it? What could he possibly want with it?

Taemon called the journal to him with psi, zipped the bag closed, then curled up in his corner and tried to think what to do next. Should he put the journal back and hope that Yens returned it? Or should he hold on to it and risk a confrontation once Yens realized it was missing? He thought back to Yens's outburst the night before. He didn't want to risk that again. Even so, Taemon's fingers still itched to draw. Yens already knew that Taemon could drive the unisphere; what harm could there be in sketching the parts he'd seen?

He opened the journal to begin drawing. But rather than seeing his neat, blocky handwriting and his sketches, he saw spiky, awkward letters on the page.

T drove a unisphere. said he never saw one before but
he knew how to drive it. how? it has to be a mind trick

of some kind but he doesn't even know what it is or
what it can do. i should have it. i will have it. it can't
be that hard. i will make him tell me how he does it
and i will be the true son. yens the true son.

Skies! It was Yens's journal. The one he said he'd thrown away. Yens wanted to learn mind wandering? How would that help him be selected as the True Son? Didn't he know how dangerous it was?

He flipped through the previous pages. The entries spanned several months. It seemed like Yens was experimenting with psi, looking for ways to get around the safeguards, ways to be more powerful.

danger increases power, but fear weakens it. facing
danger without fear gives the most power. authority
doesn't matter anymore.

Taemon slipped the journal back into Yens's suitcase and zipped it up. It took longer than it should have because the whirling thoughts in his head made it difficult to focus enough to use psi. He thought again about what had happened on the unisphere last night. Yens had purposefully put himself and Taemon in danger in order to expand his psionic power. How many people could do that? How many people *would* do that? Skies, Yens had the icy nerve of a jaguar.

Still, Taemon shuddered to think how wrong that was. Authority doesn't matter? Your own brother's *life* doesn't matter? Was that the big change that the next Great Cycle would bring? He wasn't sure he wanted to live in a place where psi had no boundaries and where power was more important than people's lives.

Worry tightened Taemon's chest. Yens was determined to seek out danger in more ways than one. And no matter what the goal was, Yens always scored.

At the beach, Taemon walked the path that followed the rocky shoreline, hoping for a few minutes alone—and something to distract him from his confused thoughts about Yens. He had a school project he was supposed to work on over the summer, and he needed some ideas. The assignment was to design your own psi lock for your locker. The lock had to be unique so that only its maker knew how it worked. Unlocking it meant picturing the mechanism releasing, then using psi to make it happen.

Make it too simple and anyone could figure out how to unlock it. Make it too complicated and even the maker might have trouble holding the release image in his head. The assignment wasn't that hard, but this was the kind of thing Taemon loved puzzling out. He wanted to create something truly original.

Da always said the best inspiration comes from nature. Taemon walked over to the knee-high stone wall that ran along the sandy path, just high enough to keep someone from accidentally falling off. Looking over the ledge, he saw the ocean a few feet down and wondered how it might help him design a lock.

Waves.

Rocks.

Crashing.

He'd been lucky to avoid a crash last night. Maybe he could use something from the unisphere's design for his lock. Maybe . . .

"Dare you to jump in right here," Yens said.

Taemon turned around. Yens had crept up next to him. Once again Taemon found himself right where he didn't want to be—alone with Yens.

"C'mon, freakling. Jump in," Yens repeated.

The water didn't look too bad. He was a good swimmer. He could probably do it. The problem was that Yens would turn it into something else, something dangerous. Taemon stepped away from the edge and back to the path. "Nah," he said.

"Right," Yens said. "Let's go for a walk instead because that's so much more exciting."

Yens was bored. And a bored Yens was a dangerous Yens.

Taemon kept walking. Both boys were quiet for the next few minutes, Taemon keeping to himself and Yens poking the sand with a stick. Then Yens began walking on top of the rocky ledge.

Taemon watched his brother out of the corner of his eye. It made him nervous to see Yens flirting with danger again, but he was certain that's exactly what Yens wanted. If he ignored him, maybe Yens would give up. It wasn't easy, though, with Yens pretending to stagger and stumble, leaning this way and that with a smirky grin on his face.

"Whoa," Yens said, teetering dramatically. He waved his arms to gain balance.

Taemon looked away.

"Whoa!" Yens called, more loudly this time. Taemon rolled his eyes and looked back—just in time to see Yens teeter toward the edge and then disappear over the wall.

Was it a trick? It must be. Taemon waited for Yens to jump out or yell or anything.

Nothing happened.

Taemon wouldn't go near the edge. He wasn't going to fall for Yens's prank. He waited several minutes, listening to the surge of the surf, the cries of the gulls. Another several minutes. Nothing.

What if something had happened to Yens? Shouldn't he check, at least? Just one tiny look. He walked over to the ledge, planted his feet solidly on the ground, and peeked over the wall.

And there was Yens. Crouched on a rock on the other side. His laughter was loud and cocky.

"Got you that time!"

"I had to check on you, that's all."

Yens climbed up the rocks toward the wall. Taemon helped Yens up with a little psi boost. Before he realized what was happening, Taemon felt himself being yanked forward, his belly pinned to the stone wall. He hung there, head on the ocean side of the wall and feet on the other, slowly tipping forward.

"Let's go for a swim," Yens said with a snarl.

"Stop it, Yens." Yens shouldn't be able to use psi to hurt anyone, especially his own brother. But after reading his brother's journal, Taemon was beginning to think that Yens was capable of just about anything.

"Tell me how you drove the unisphere."

Taemon's head was pounding, and the stone wall jamming in his gut made it hard to get a good breath. "Skies! Is power all you care about?"

Yens's face contorted into an odd scowl. Taemon felt a shove of psi and toppled over the wall. A shower of pebbles escorted him into the water below.

The water was warm, but it was strong and deep. The small waves on the surface hid an incredible force that shoved and pulled at Taemon as he tried to swim to shore. The water tugged him outward, then thrust him back toward the rocks and jammed him against a boulder. Before Taemon could climb the rock, he was thrust outward again by the sea.

He wondered how fast he was moving. Fast enough to break a bone if he hit the rocks wrong? *Don't panic,*

Taemon told himself. *Focus on breathing.* The water would eventually push him back toward the rock, where he'd have another chance to climb out.

And it did. Taemon tried to keep himself aligned so his feet would hit the rocks first. Better his legs get broken than something indispensable like his head. He glanced up and saw Yens standing on the boulder. He breathed a bit easier.

Taemon's feet hit the boulder just as he'd planned. He bent his knees to cushion the impact, and nothing broke. Swinging his arms forward, he managed to hug the boulder, but his toes found no footholds. He scrabbled for purchase on the smooth, slippery rock. "Help me!"

Taemon felt psi pulling at his shoulders. His body started to lift out of the water. Relief washed over him.

Just before Taemon could get to a safe position, his forward momentum stopped. He hung suspended above the rock.

"Tell me how you worked the unisphere," Yens said. "Then I'll help you."

"I told you, I don't know! I just saw it. I can't explain how!"

"Try."

The waves returned, engulfing Taemon from the waist down and pressing him up against the rock. He fought to breathe.

"If I concentrate," he began, knowing that he had no choice, "I can search things with my mind. See how they work. But I don't know how I do it! I just do. Da said never to tell anyone. He said it's dangerous!"

"Dangerous for you. But I know what to do with it."

"Forget all this stuff about danger increasing power. You're asking for disaster."

Yens grinned. "That's the whole point." And he let go.

Taemon fell into the water, and the sea hauled him out again.

3 WATER

As Monkey sees its final hour,
Water bursts in like a shower,
Calming, cleansing, and renewing,
Pounding, crashing, and undoing.
You must understand its power.
You must understand its power.

— CALENDAR SONG

Once more Taemon fought to position himself for another chance to climb onto the rocks. But this time he felt something different. This time the ocean pulled him sideways. Not much, but it meant he'd end up someplace other than the big boulder. Maybe a better place to climb out. Maybe worse. No way to know.

Sure enough, when Taemon was pushed back to shore, he missed the boulder by a few feet. Yens was yelling something, but Taemon couldn't make it out.

Here the rocks were submerged under the churning sea. He couldn't see them, but he could feel them scraping his knees and shins. He had to find someplace safer.

In the rocks he *could* see, there was a gap that caught his eye. Maybe that would lead to a way out. He tried to aim toward it.

It worked. Taemon reached the gap. No more hidden rocks smashing into his body. But it wasn't just a gap. The sea pushed him into a cave the size of his living room.

At least he was safe. He'd rest here awhile and swim out in a few minutes. It should be easy. He would figure out the timing of the water's pull and use it to help him swim out of the cave. With his strength back, he should be able to aim himself at the boulder once again. He needed to rest a bit, that's all. Catch his breath.

Taemon waded through the shallow water to the back of the cave and found a ledge that he could sit on, the water up to his waist. As his breathing slowed, he looked around at this strange hidden place. Sunlight poured in from the opening and reflected off the water, throwing beams of light in various directions on the cave walls, and creating rippled rainbows.

Taemon wasn't sure how much time had passed, but

the water was up to his chest now and he figured it was time to swim out. He concentrated on the rhythm of the waves and timed his swimming to match it. He swam toward the opening, but the ocean's pull was deceiving. When the water's direction changed, he found himself pinned against the wall of the cave.

He soon realized that swimming out of the cave was going to be anything but easy. If he swam as hard as he could, he could manage to get a little way out of the cave, but the sea battered him against the rocks and eventually pushed him right back in, with several new bruises for his efforts. Taemon was exhausted. He swam to the ledge again to rest.

The rainbow-black walls didn't look so wonderful now. As he sat on the ledge with the water up to his shoulders, the push and pull of the ocean was much stronger now in the deeper water. He had to wedge himself into places where the rock jutted out so that the current wouldn't toss him about. He sat there, resting as much as he dared, willing himself to relax and think.

He was not strong enough to swim out of the cave. That much was certain. Would Yens go for help? Had anyone else seen him fall? He waited and rested.

Was it his imagination, or was the water rising faster? It was up to his chin. He tried to stand on the ledge, but the ceiling was too low on this side. If he stood, he had to bend over, which meant his head was not any higher. He'd have to find a way out before the water was over his head. He'd have to use psi. But how?

Was there any way out that didn't involve swimming? Taemon looked around, but he could see nothing beyond the dark walls and rising water.

Skies! He was going to have to do the mind wandering again.

He closed his eyes and tried to calm his whole body. He let his awareness follow the walls and roof of the cave. He could sense every nook and cranny—there was no other way out.

Time to change tactics. He tried to stop the rise of the water, which worked for a little while, but the effort quickly exhausted him. He tried pushing the ocean water back out of the cave, manipulating rocks to block the opening—anything he could think of to buy more time. But psi had its limitations. Everything Taemon tried to move was just too heavy. He had to find something smaller to manipulate. And he had to do it fast.

Now he had to tilt his head backward to breathe. Salty water sloshed around his nose and mouth.

He fought fear. Fear would only diminish his psi. *Think. Relax.* All right, so the water would soon be over his head. Could he use psi to breathe water instead of air? It seemed the only option.

Taemon had never attempted using psi on himself. He'd heard plenty of stories of people who had done such things, and the results were always harmful, often fatal. Healers knew how to do certain things for the body, but even trained professionals would never attempt psi healing on themselves. It was much too risky. Knowledge of the human body was restricted to healers and midwives, so Taemon knew little of how breathing worked or even why it was necessary.

But he had to try something. It had come down to a choice of risky psi or certain death.

So Taemon let his mind wander again, only this time, he sent his awareness inside himself. Taking a big gulp of air, he focused on his breath and followed where it went. He sensed a breathing tube that ran down his neck and split into two spongy places inside his chest. The sponges rose and fell as Taemon breathed. He continued his exploration. The air passageway branched off into narrower and narrower tubes, each of which dead-ended in a tiny air sac.

Something was happening here. He didn't know the words to describe it, but he could tell that part of the air was moving into the sac. His body seemed to need only a certain part of the air, not all of it. But which part?

Taking another breath, Taemon sent his awareness in closer to explore exactly what was happening. When he thought he understood, he exhaled. The air backtracked all the way out of his chest and bubbled through his nose.

Now he knew he needed a certain kind of air particle. He only had a few minutes before normal breathing would become impossible. Could he get these little particles from water, or were they only found in air?

He reached out with his mind to look for this certain little particle his body needed for breathing. There were so many strange little things in the water, and they all looked different. Where were the little bits he needed to breathe?

Wait. Yes! Those breathing bits were there, but tangled up with a bunch of others. It was just like the colored building rods he used to play with when he was first learning psi. Those little breathing particles would have to be separated from the water, then recombined into something his body could use for air.

Carefully, Taemon drew a little water into his mouth. He sent his mind scurrying to tag all the tiny parts he needed. The next part was tricky. Taemon connected with all those little bits at the same time. He pictured a specific image in his mind in which all the tagged bits combined into breathable air and moved down to his air sacs while everything else moved out of his mouth.

With a controlled burst of psi, Taemon sent the order. *Be it so!*

And it worked. Bubbles came out of his mouth and the right bits of air went down toward his chest. The first few breaths tickled and caught in his throat, like a hiccup gone wrong. Each breath felt a little smoother.

He could do it. He had to concentrate harder than ever before. He had to relax more than ever before. He had to control his psi more than ever before. But he could do it.

Taemon lay on the ledge, completely submerged now. Good bits in, bad bits out. That alone took all his attention. He fell into a kind of trance as he focused so closely on breathing. *Good bits in, bad bits out. Good bits in, bad bits out.*

Time passed, maybe minutes, maybe hours—Taemon had no idea.

When his awareness returned, someone was lifting him out of the water. This person was saying something, wanting Taemon to respond. He was too weak to answer. He was utterly exhausted—almost entirely drained of energy.

He was out of the water.

He was alive.

4 WIND

After Water drains away,

Wind blows in to rule the day.

A breeze can freshen, lift, and change.

A gust can ruin, rearrange.

For good or ill, Wind has its way.

For good or ill, Wind has its way.

— CALENDAR SONG

"How long was he in the cave?" a woman's voice asked.

"Nearly an hour," Da said.

"Underwater all that time?"

Taemon opened his eyes just enough to see where he was and who was talking. He was home, in his room. And the woman wore the medallion of a healer. He closed his eyes again and pretended to sleep.

"We're not sure," Da said. "When the divers finally found him, he was lying underwater."

"Does it matter?" Mam said. "Obviously he didn't drown. There must have been air pockets or some such thing." Her voice sounded strained and tense. Mam had always been overprotective of him and Yens. Da said it was on account of her younger sister dying when Mam was only six. The sea cave incident must have thrown her to new levels of panic.

"Still, I'd try to downplay that part of the incident," said the healer.

"He hasn't told us anything about what happened," Da said. "We felt it best not to push him."

"How much does he sleep?" the healer asked.

"He wakes up every few hours with a huge appetite," Mam said. "He eats, then sleeps again."

"Appetite. That's good," the healer said. "But we'll need to watch for signs of possible brain damage."

"He's fine," Mam said sharply. "He just needs time to recuperate."

"That's possible, too. My point is, keep a close eye on him. If you notice anything unusual, any loss of psi, let me know. I'll check back with you before Sabbath."

"That won't be necessary," Mam said. "His psi is perfectly fine."

"I'll check back with you," said the healer. Taemon heard her walk out of the room.

"Renda," whispered Da, "we can trust her. We might need her help again."

"Shh!" Mam's voice was barely audible. "Things are different now. She's under a lot of pressure to report things like this."

Mam and Da left the room, too.

Taemon opened his eyes again to make sure everyone had gone. Brain damage? Loss of psi? No wonder Mam sounded worried.

He reached out with psi to move his bedcovers. The sheet and blankets flew back instantly. Using psi felt easier than ever, more natural.

What a relief. Taemon knew what happened to people who didn't have any psi. They were sent away. The nice name for that place was the powerless colony; the cruel name was the dud farm. It wasn't safe for feebleminded people to be with normal people. They were slow and vulnerable, they couldn't do any work, and they were unstable.

He thought about getting up, but even thinking about it made him tired. Two days had passed since the sea cave, and still he was worn out. He used psi to pull the covers over him again, then rolled over and drifted back to sleep.

He woke again, hungry. Famished. He stood up, woozy at first. With each wobbly step, he felt a bit more steady.

Chimes on the back porch jingled with the wind. Taemon smelled food and headed downstairs.

Mam stood in the kitchen with her back to Taemon. She stacked the dishes with psi. Coral-colored sunlight streamed through the windows. Was it dusk or dawn? Dinner or breakfast?

"Can I have something to eat?" Taemon asked.

"Oh!" Mam turned quickly, and a plate shattered on the floor. "You shouldn't be up!" She rushed over and lifted his chin with psi, then looked into his eyes. "Are you all right? How do you feel?"

Awful, he wanted to say, but didn't. She worried enough as it was. Even so, as Mam studied his face, he found himself wishing she would . . . what? What was it he needed from her? He didn't know, but a concerned look wasn't it.

"Just hungry," said Taemon. "Sorry about the plate."

"Don't worry about that." Mam smiled, then turned

toward the dishes and started filling a plate. "He's hungry," she said to no one in particular. "Of course he's hungry. He's fine, just like I said. Fit as a fig. What do healers know?" She used psi to ruffle Taemon's hair in the way he didn't like.

The food smells hung in the kitchen, and Taemon's stomach rumbled. "So . . . I can have something to eat?"

"Something to eat! Yes, yes. Now, Taemon, you mustn't rush things. Back to bed with you. I'll bring you a plate in just a few minutes." Dishes and food and broken plate pieces slid into their places as Mam used psi to tidy up. She hummed as she worked.

Taemon padded back to his room.

A food tray came floating in, laden with sliced pineapple, steamed grain, and shepherd's cheese. Food! Finally! "Thanks, Mam," Taemon said.

The tray settled itself on Taemon's lap. With his psi, he lifted a huge bite toward his mouth.

But it wasn't Mam who followed the food tray into Taemon's room. It was Yens. "So, how's the miracle boy?"

He hadn't talked to Yens since the accident—if it really was an accident—and he wasn't about to start now. He didn't know what to say, and he was too hungry to talk. All he wanted was the food.

Taemon looked down at his plate as he chewed. He drew a hunk of cheese into his mouth. He couldn't get it into his stomach fast enough.

Yens sat on the chair next to Taemon's bed. "No one's ever survived the Demon's Maw. That's what the cave is called, you know. Demon's Maw." Yens leaned forward. "How'd you do it, freakling?"

Taemon started in on the pineapple. What he'd done, with the seawater, with the breathing, it was definitely bad psi. People weren't supposed to use psi outside their authority, beyond their training. He could get in big trouble if they found out he could do things like that. Locked up, maybe. Da would have a fit. Mam would . . . Mam would . . .

No. He couldn't tell anyone. Especially not Yens.

Without warning, the plate lurched from Taemon's lap and hovered close to Yens.

"I'll eat and you talk," Yens said, taking a large bite of pineapple. "Now tell me how you kept yourself alive. It was mind wandering, wasn't it? Tell me how you did it."

Taemon looked at the food as Yens ate. His body screamed for more. He wanted that food. *Needed* it.

"Tell me what happened, then I'll give you the food." Yens spoke with his mouth full. "If there's any left."

"I almost died because of you. Twice. Put yourself in danger if you want, but leave me out of it."

Yens laughed, pineapple juice dribbling down his chin. "I'm the one who brought the rescuers. I'm the reason you *didn't* die." He took a bite of Taemon's cheese.

All at once, it was too much to bear. The hunger, the anger, the fatigue. Taemon pressed his mouth into a tight line. His breath came noisy and fast. Before he realized it, he had snatched the plate away and pressed Yens and his chair up against the wall, all done with lightning-fast psi.

Yens had been taken by surprise, which Taemon hoped would give him a few seconds before Yens could clear his mind enough to fight back.

Taemon looked Yens in the eye. "No one is going to use mind wandering. Not you. Not me."

Yens matched Taemon's stare and gave a little shrug. "Fine. Next time, I let you die."

That shrug. It was infuriating. Taemon had let out a little anger, and now all of it wanted out. "You want to know what happened in the cave? You want to know how I survived?" he said. "I'll show you."

He reached out with all his psi toward Yens. In an instant, he found Yens's breathing tube and followed it down all the way to the tiny air sacs. Then he connected with the air particles in Yens's chest. He pictured the air blowing like wind. Blowing up and out of Yens's mouth, emptying the tiny sacs. *Be it so!* Tameon ordered.

Yens gaped like a dying fish. His eyes widened with fear.

Taemon remembered his terror inside the sea cave. Fear. Helplessness. Exhaustion. He wanted Yens to feel every bit of that. Yens fell off the chair and onto the floor. He lay curled in a ball, trembling.

"That's what it was like," Taemon said. Let Yens figure out a way to live without breathing. Let Yens feel death tugging on his sleeve.

But as he watched Yens struggle to breathe, questions and doubts swirled in Taemon's head. How was this possible? Taemon shouldn't be able to use psi against Yens unless he was defending himself or assisting him, and he certainly wasn't showing affection. How was he able to attack his brother like this when he was clearly acting outside his authority? Wasn't this the same thing

Yens had been experimenting with? But why could Taemon do it?

A voice—a female voice—he had never heard before spoke in Taemon's mind. It was calm and clear.

Your thoughts are true. Your brother has chosen selfishness, greed, and ambition. Pride clouds his vision, whereas your humility allows you to see truth.

Scenes flashed in Taemon's mind. Yens looking down at the lifeless body of a pretty girl. Yens tearing buildings apart. Yens ordering armies into battle.

You have authority to end his life.

End his life? This was madness! This was forbidden!

This is truth, the voice said. **I give the authority.**

Taemon looked at Yens. His face was blue. His eyes were wild. Worst of all, Taemon was glad.

Part of him wanted to obey the voice. It would be so easy. No one would know Taemon had killed him. Yens could have easily choked on the food he was cramming down.

Taemon felt his psi gathering. Gathering, building, waiting for the order.

The order to kill.

Skies, what was he thinking? If ever there was bad psi,

this was it! Yens's face turned from blue to purple, and the psi inside Taemon screamed to be released. He felt dizzy—dizzy with power, with the significance of his choice. Dizzy with fear.

There was only one choice if he didn't want to kill Yens. Hardly a choice at all. He fixed his mind on what he wanted.

Be it so!

The order came from some deep part of Taemon, beneath awareness and reason. Someplace where survival was all that mattered.

Taemon's body trembled as a vast amount of psi left him. Over the ringing in his ears he heard Yens gasp deep breaths. He watched as the color returned to his brother's face.

Then everything went completely dark.

5 RABBIT

Wind dies down as Rabbit rises.

He jumps and flees from all surprises.

Does he run because of fear?

Or because his life is dear?

Survival takes on many guises.

Survival takes on many guises.

— CALENDAR SONG

The first day of the new school year was only a few days away and Taemon hadn't even started his lock yet. A psi lock wasn't that hard to make. For a person with psi.

But Taemon had no psi. Not one shred. Not since the awful day one month and five days ago when he had almost killed Yens. Da was certain it was temporary, but Taemon knew differently. Somehow he had lost all connection with psi.

Taemon had thought a lot about that moment, that split second when everything changed, wondering how it had happened. He remembered wanting to kill Yens, building up a huge amount of psi, and then changing his mind. The Heart of the Earth had deemed him unworthy of psi. That was the only reason he could think of for losing it.

Maybe it was best this way. At least he didn't have to worry about hurting anyone.

Standing in Da's workshop, Taemon stared at a box full of bolts and cams and latches that might be used to make a lock. The lock was due at the end of the week. Four days left to figure out how to make a lock that didn't need psi. He let out a huff.

Da stood behind him, looking over his shoulder. "We could make something that looks like a lock, but isn't."

Taemon shook his head. "The teacher will know. She'll test it."

Mam walked in the workshop. "Any progress?"

"Not yet." Taemon sighed.

"I can talk to your new teacher," Da said. "I'll tell her you're still upset about the accident."

Taemon shook his head.

"We'll tell her that you have trouble using psi in front of people," Mam said. "We'll tell her you're really shy and—"

"No," Taemon said. Would they ever stop treating him like a baby? They seemed to think that being power-less was the same as being an infant. "I'm going to figure something out. Some way to trick them."

Mam and Da exchanged a look. Da placed a hand on Taemon's shoulder. He shrugged it off.

"Son," Da said, "it's time to find your psi again. You have it inside you somewhere. All you need is confidence. Just because Yens's psi is so strong doesn't mean—"

"Can we please not talk about Yens?" Taemon said. Since the accident, Yens's psionic ability had skyrocketed. All that experimenting he'd done must have paid off. Or maybe Taemon's weakness gave Yens more confidence. Whatever the reason, Yens was beginning to really stand out. He'd been named captain of his psiball team. He'd taken the golden urn at the young musicians' festival. All this while Taemon was trying to figure out how to zip his own fly without asking Mam to do it for him.

"You might as well accept it," Taemon said to Da. "I have no psi. None."

"Shh!" The door slammed shut with Mam's psi. "If someone heard that, you'd be carted off before first light."

Taemon frowned. "Don't worry: no one will know. I've faked it this far, haven't I?"

It was true. In just four weeks, Taemon had learned to deceive neighbors, friends, and people at church. Sleight-of-hand tricks worked well. And magnets often came in handy.

Most people figured he was clumsy and slow since the accident. No one seemed to suspect that Taemon was powerless. Probably because no one had ever spent much time around a powerless person. The only disabled people in the city were the dozen or so that lived and worked in the temple. They were innocents, powerless people who didn't know anything different. No one spoke to them or saw them outside the temple.

"You can't fake everything," Da said. "What about lunch at school? You can't eat in front of anyone."

"I've already thought of that," Taemon said. "I'll spend lunch in my classroom doing schoolwork. I'll need more time to do my assignments anyway. I can eat when I get home."

"Still, I'm not sure you can pull this off," Da said. "We should work on finding your psi."

"It's not like I've misplaced it," Taemon said, frustrated. "It's *gone*." Completely. His parents thought his disability was due to the trauma of near drowning, and he'd never told them anything different. He'd never told them how he'd become unworthy of psi. Being powerless was a shameful thing—more so, even, than being a liar and a cheat. But at least he wasn't dangerous anymore.

Skies, but this lock assignment had him stumped. "Just leave me alone and let me figure this out," he told his parents.

Most of the time, Taemon was allowed to eat alone in his bedroom where he could use his hands all he wanted. At dinner, Mam insisted that they eat together. "We're still a family," she'd said, "and families eat together."

But that did not mean Taemon was permitted the use of his hands at the dinner table. Mam used her psi to hold his food up for him to eat, as she had done when he was a baby. He felt a wave of humiliation with every bite.

Tonight, Da was quiet and broody, though Yens seemed to be in a good mood. Maybe they could have an argument-free meal for once.

Yens cleared his throat. "Today is a great day for the Houser family."

Mam looked nervously at Da. The caramelized cucumber in front of Taemon dropped to his plate. He couldn't pick it up. Short of lowering his head to his plate like a dog, he couldn't eat until Mam picked up his food for him.

Cucumbers were no big loss. He didn't even like them. What he'd really like to do is tuck into that lamb roll.

Yens leaned back in his chair and clasped his hands behind his neck. In spite of himself, Taemon was curious about what Yens was going to announce. What was it this time? Had his exhibit for the nature fair taken first place?

Da raised his eyes from his meal with a dark look. "Boasting is not permitted in this house." Da was always firm about the sin of pride. The scriptures said pride would be the downfall of the true people. Da took that seriously.

Taemon stared at the food on his plate. As hungry as he was, he didn't dare pick it up.

"Some priests came to the school today and tested a few of us." Taemon could hear the glee in Yens's voice, and the fact that the news was upsetting to Da seemed to add to it. "The results were . . . interesting." Yens let his words hang in the air for a moment for maximum effect. "They said I did things they'd never seen before."

Da buried his head in his hands.

Mam looked stunned.

Yens grinned. "Don't be surprised when they pick me as the True Son."

Calmly, Mam pushed back her chair and walked over to Yens. Taemon startled at the smacking sound that came next. Yens recoiled, and when a red spot appeared on his cheek, Taemon understood what had happened. Mam had slapped Yens's face with psi. Even though parents had authority to discipline their children with psi, Mam had never done it before. Maybe a twist of the ear now and again, but nothing like a slap.

She left the room.

Da glared at Yens. "Do you see? Do you see what this is doing to her?"

Poor Mam. She could never relax. She was Rabbit through and through, jumpy by nature. But every sign had a positive and a negative side. Mam would do anything to survive. Anything to make sure her boys weren't taken away. Yens to the temple and Taemon to the dud farm. Taemon could not control Yens—no one could—but he would make sure *he* never got sent away.

Yens showed no such concern. "Da, you're a religion teacher. You should be proud—I mean *pleased*—that I'm to be the True Son."

Da gripped the table. "It's not a contest. It isn't a prize to be won. The Heart of Earth will choose the one to begin the next Great Cycle."

"But the high priest says the True Son has been born. They're looking for someone who—"

"The high priest is looking to increase his own power," Da said. He shook his head slowly. "He only wants someone he can mold into the True Son. Someone to help him manipulate the people. If he takes you to the temple, you'll be the true puppet, nothing more."

"What is wrong with this family?" Yens stood up and left the table. As his brother stormed out of the room, Taemon noticed that the red mark on Yens's cheek was in the shape of a rabbit. Mam had left her mark, sure as sunrise.

Taemon frowned. Could Yens really be the True Son? He was powerful enough. But somehow Taemon had always thought the True Son would be different. Someone . . . good.

A new thought struck Taemon: What if he had come a breath away from killing the True Son?

Worse yet, what if he should have killed Yens in order to *prevent* him from becoming the True Son?

Skies! It was all so confusing. He'd lost his psi either because of his unworthy thoughts or because he wasn't brave enough to do what needed to be done. Did it really matter which one? Either way amounted to a massive failure.

Taemon and Yens had never spoken of what happened that day. Talking about it would mean admitting that Taemon had bested him, and Yens wouldn't do that. Just as he wouldn't say anything about his little brother being a powerless slug—not when it might mar his prospects for becoming the True Son. But once he was chosen, if he was chosen, would he still keep quiet?

Perhaps the one bright outcome of all this was that the competition between Taemon and his brother had evaporated. Yens was clearly the star in the family, and Taemon was clearly the weakling. Yens was the psiball champion, the outstanding scholar, the gifted musician. Taemon fell easily into the role of Nobody.

Mam did not come back to the table, which meant Taemon's meal was over. The cucumber lay tepid and limp on his plate, which was fine with him. But walking away from the untouched lamb roll? *That* was difficult.

Four days later, Taemon's big moment came. It was time to demonstrate his lock. Taemon had already attached it to the handle of the locker when no one was looking. He stood in the hallway and waited for the teacher. It was midmorning break. Taemon had specifically requested this time slot to complete his lock assignment. He hoped the people milling around in the hall would distract the teacher. And Taemon needed all the distractions he could get.

The lock worked at home, but could he do it in front of the teacher? Was it good enough to fool her? Or would he wake up tomorrow at the dud farm?

The teacher walked up and stood next to Taemon. She leaned forward, peering at the lock. "It certainly has a . . . unique design."

"Um, thank you," said Taemon. "That's what I intended."

Was it too different? Would it stand out too much? He'd soon find out.

Tilting the lock upward with her psi, the teacher peered at it and frowned. "This slot on the bottom . . . what's it for?"

"I . . . don't want to be rude but . . . I'd rather not explain."

The teacher sniffed. "Yes, well, I suppose that's the point of a lock, to make it incomprehensible to others."

Taemon exhaled. "Exactly."

He slid in between the teacher and the lock. He couldn't afford to have her scrutinize it any further.

With a gentle nudge of psi, she turned Taemon around to face the locker. "All right. Let's see you unlock it."

"The thing is . . ." He leaned forward and whispered, "I can do it better if I turn my back to the lock."

He knew this was risky. It didn't make sense to turn your back on the object you were manipulating with psi. But he felt sure he could do a better job diverting the teacher's attention if he could face her, make eye contact with her.

"What is your name again? Tymon?"

"TAY-mon."

"Well, Taemon, using psi means influencing an object's spatial positioning. To do that, we must make mental contact with the object. And mental contact begins with visual contact."

"Right. I know that's how most people do it. I don't know why, but it's easier for me if I turn my back."

"Try it my way first." The teacher pressed her lips into a tight line.

"Okay." Taemon faced the locker and pretended to concentrate. He stared at the lock for a few seconds. Predictably, nothing happened.

"Please," said Taemon. "If I could just turn around."

The teacher sniffed again. "Most unorthodox. No visual contact? People have to train years for that kind of psi."

Taemon's heart pounded. Unorthodox wasn't good, but it was flaming better than the truth. He held his breath.

"Well, I suppose there's nothing in the assignment that requires visual contact." The teacher sighed. "Go ahead: give it a try."

Taemon exhaled. He turned around so his back was to the locker. Now came the tricky part. He needed her to look away from the lock. He stretched one hand forward and curled his fingers as if holding an invisible ball. Holding that pose, he made his hand tremble slightly.

It seemed to work. The teacher looked confused. More important, she was staring at his shaking hand. With his other hand, Taemon reached behind his back.

He fixed a look of concentration on his face and cocked his head, just as he'd seen weak kids do many times. An experienced psi wielder never contorted his face at all. Any grimace, gesture, or grunt was the clumsy sign of a novice.

Taemon's act seemed to be working. The teacher was observing his facial expressions, his hand movement. She wasn't looking at the lock at all.

Staring straight ahead, Taemon kept up the trembling hand act. With his hidden hand, he turned his wrist until a small metal rod slipped out of his sleeve and into his hand. He forced the metal rod into the slot in the lock, just as he'd practiced.

Click!

In one smooth motion, he turned sideways and slipped the metal rod into his pocket—on the side hidden from the teacher. He relaxed. "There."

"Indeed." The teacher stepped forward and checked the lock. She looked up and glared at Taemon. "Well, young man, I'm not sure what to make of you. Do I put you in the advanced group because you didn't need visual contact? Or in the beginner group because of the hand movement?"

Taemon smiled. He didn't care which group he was in; he was just glad to be in.

Once the teacher turned and walked away, Taemon glanced around to be sure no one was looking, then quickly closed the lock again and headed toward his classroom.

In the hall, people stared at him and whispered.

"Did you see the way his hand trembled?"

"What a freakling."

"Isn't that Yens Houser's brother?"

"How can a psiball champion have a weak freak for a brother?"

Taemon kept his head down and picked up his pace. He'd heard all that before. It didn't bother him. Much.

"A psiless lock. Pure genius!"

He stopped cold, then turned around to see who had caught him cheating.

6 SERPENT

Serpent scares the hare away
And slithers in to start his day.
Be on your guard, for he's deceptive.
But snakes can also be protective.
For Serpent has a forceful way.
For Serpent has a forceful way.

— CALENDAR SONG

Taemon searched the faces in the hallway for the one who'd spoken. A boy with black hair that flopped partly over his eyes stepped forward. Taemon looked closely at those eyes. Was there menace there, or only morbid curiosity?

The boy stared back at Taemon. "I'm not sure if I want you around me. Now I can't be the resident weak freak anymore." He smiled wryly.

Weak freak. Taemon winced at the term, but that's exactly what he needed people to think he was. Weaklings were teased, ridiculed, bullied, but they weren't sent away. What better way to appear weak than to sling around with the weaklings?

"Cha. I've got you beat, all right. I'm Taemon. Birth sign's Quake."

"Moke," said the boy. "Serpent."

The sign of the serpent could mean deception, or it could mean protection. So this Moke was either hiding something or providing a safeguard. Taemon shifted his weight. Maybe making friends wasn't such a good idea. He might get too comfortable around friends, too careless.

"You don't know what to make of me." Moke nodded. "That's okay: you're a Quake after all. Quakes are supposed to question. Here's what you need to know before you decide: My parents run the crematorium. I study weasel droppings. I create sculptures from cat hair. And I stink at psiball."

Taemon laughed. "I stink at psiball, too."

"Excellent," the boy said. "We can be partners. We'll stink the pants off everybody."

Two days later, Taemon was in Moke's backyard, sitting on the edge of a half-sphere. At fifteen feet in diameter, the metal half-sphere glinted in the autumn afternoon sunlight like a giant silver bowl. Real psiball matches were played in a full sphere made of lead crystal, but those were expensive and running the crematorium didn't exactly make Moke's family rich. Families like Taemon's and Moke's could never afford a crystal psiball sphere, but a metal half-sphere at least gave them something to practice on.

The half-sphere had four holes evenly spaced around its equator. A full sphere had a hole at the very top as well. Four players, two teams of two, stood inside the sphere, where they used their psi to direct the ball into one of the holes. To score a point, a team had to get control of the ball, turn the edge of the hole the color of their team, and send the ball through the hole, all done with psi.

"So what's your plan for stinking the pants off everybody?" Taemon asked.

"The way I figure it," Moke said, "we have to turn our weakness into strength."

Taemon rolled his eyes. "You sound like my da. 'The way to deal with weakness is to get stronger.'"

"Did I say anything about getting stronger? I'm talking about using our weakness."

Taemon frowned. "I don't get it."

Moke pushed off the edge of the half-sphere and landed at the bottom of the bowl. "Okay. Let's pretend we don't have any psi at all."

Taemon stiffened. Sometimes Moke seemed to know that Taemon was powerless. Or maybe it was just the guilty feeling that made it seem like people knew.

"I know. It sounds stupid, right? I mean, how could you play psiball without any psi at all?" Moke said. "But just think about it. How *would* you play without psi?"

"Well, I guess you'd have to—"

Moke beckoned with a toss of his head. "Show me."

Taemon jumped into the half-sphere beside Moke, the ball resting at the bottom. It was about the size of a person's head and covered with black leather, heavy and soft enough that it didn't roll or bounce on its own. Moke had painted his birth sign, Serpent, on the ball.

"You'd have to push it with your foot or something."

Moke nodded. "Let's see you try."

With the side of his foot, Taemon kicked the ball up along the inside curve of the half-sphere. They took turns until both of them had found the right amount of force to send the ball through one of the holes.

"What about changing the hole's color?" Taemon asked. "We can't do that without psi." Because the ball is moved with psi, the spectators and referees couldn't tell who was controlling the ball. In order to score a point, the players had to use psi to turn the perimeter of the hole their team's color.

"Yeah, we'll have to use a little psi for the colors. No getting around that, I suppose." Moke rubbed his chin. "Shouldn't be a problem. Coloring the hole is the easy part."

"Maybe for you," Taemon said. "I'm color-blind." It was another lie, of course. Add it to the list.

"Powerless and color-blind. You take weakling to a new level, my friend." Moke kicked the ball into the east hole.

Taemon tried to laugh it off. "If you're going to be a weakling, be the best. That's my motto."

Moke used a squinch of psi to clap Taemon on the shoulder. "We're doing this for all the weaklings out there. We're going to show them that weaklings can have fun and be clever, too."

"I guess," Taemon mumbled. He wondered how weak Moke really was or if he just enjoyed being different.

"Spoken like a true weakling," said Moke. "Now let's get back to work."

"Absolutely not," Da said. "I forbid it."

Mam looked up from her embroidery. "Maybe we should hear him out."

The bright yellow embroidery floss kept looping and pulling, looping and pulling, as a bird took shape on the red cloth.

The house was quiet in the dusky hours before sleep. Yens was out in Da's workshop, practicing his music. Taemon had decided this was as good a time as any to bring up psiball. He'd closed the shutters tight so no one could overhear.

Da drew a sip of coffee from his mug on the table. Like a dark thread, it disappeared into his mouth. He nodded for Taemon to continue.

"I have a psiball partner. His name is Moke. We've been practicing and—"

Da shook his head. "You can't play psiball without psi. Your partner will know you're not using psi."

"No. I mean, yes, he does, but . . . see, he doesn't have much psi, either," he said, glossing over the fact that he, himself, had *none*. "So we decided to try this really weird thing where we only use a little psi to color the holes. It's pretty klonky, but it works. Sort of."

"Psiball without psi?" Mam looked baffled. "What's the point of that?"

"The point is to show that we can do it. That you don't need psi to be good at something. Besides, nothing in the rules actually says you have to use psi. With no psi, the strategies are completely different. We're counting on the element of surprise. Because the other team will have no idea what we're doing." Taemon shrugged. "And it's fun."

"Ridiculous," Da said. "Safer to stay out of the psiball leagues altogether." He drew another sip of coffee.

Mam stopped her embroidery. "We should think carefully about this. On one hand, playing psiball will help you seem normal."

The unspoken statement was impossible to miss—he wasn't normal. It pained him to hear his own mother say it, but he couldn't argue. He would never be normal again.

Da shook his head. "But playing psiball without psi *isn't* normal. It'll cause a stir, draw attention. You'd do better to—"

A knock at the door ended the discussion.

"Who . . . ?" Mam's embroidery dropped to the table. "Good Earth, did they hear anything?"

Da used psi to open the shutter just enough to look through the window. His face turned white. He looked at Mam with apology in his eyes as he opened the door.

A man stood on the porch.

Taemon knew exactly who he was.

Elder Naseph, the high priest.

7 STONE

Stone rolls in to take control

While Serpent slinks back in his hole.

Stone is steady, firm, and stable,

Ever loyal, staunch, and faithful.

But obstinacy takes its toll.

But obstinacy takes its toll.

— CALENDAR SONG

"May I enter?" asked Elder Naseph. His tone made it clear there was only one way to answer that question.

Mam lifted a trembling hand toward her neck.

Da stepped aside silently, allowing the high priest to walk in, his chin lifted, eyes half closed, shoulders pulled back. He wore robes embroidered with intricate patterns and colors so bright Taemon had to squint to look at him. Woven into the fabric were hundreds of ornaments—beads, medallions, gems, pendants—tokens of religious status. Even his long beard jangled with trinkets.

Taemon thought of all the times Da had warned of a haughty countenance. Here, standing in their living room, was haughtiness personified.

Da turned to Taemon. "Excuse us please, son?"

Taemon left the room. The door closed behind him, likely by Mam. He hurried to the furnace room in the basement. With any luck, he'd be able to hear something through the air vents. He stood under the large duct, where he knew the voices from the living room would carry.

"—your son," Elder Naseph said.

"Which one?" asked Da.

This evoked a soft chuckle from the old sage. "The eldest."

Taemon leaned against the cellar's stone wall, listening for a scream, a gasp, the sound of Mam collapsing. He heard nothing.

The next noise was the back door opening and slamming, along with Yens's voice. "Mam! Da! Wait till—Oh. Hello, Elder Naseph. Good wishes." His words were buttery smooth.

"My son is not the True Son," Da said calmly.

"Perhaps not. But he shows great promise. Still, we will test him. Train him. A decision will be made."

"Da, please. It's my duty. I want to do everything I can for the people."

"Nothing good will come of this, Yens. Can't you see they're just—?"

"I'd be very cautious about how you finish that sentence, Brother Willjamen. Very cautious." The high priest's voice took on a threatening tone: "You would do well to remember that we have been watching both your sons. Today we leave one son with you. If you decide to challenge the authority of the church, we may decide not to be so generous."

Taemon thought he heard a gasp that must have come from Mam.

Did the high priest know about Taemon's condition? He must. And he was using it to control Da's objections. Taemon sat on the floor and hugged his knees. Being powerless hadn't erased the danger he posed to his family after all, only shifted it.

"It's the right thing, Da. I'm going." Taemon heard excitement in Yens's voice.

And from Da, silence. Da, the Stone.

The high priest told Yens he was not allowed to bring

anything with him. Taemon thought he should stay downstairs until they called for him, but that never happened. By the time he decided to go upstairs anyway, Yens was gone.

That night, Taemon pulled his copy of the scriptures from under his bed. He hadn't read the True Son prophecies for a long time. What exactly did they say? Could it really be Yens?

> And the True Son shall be the blade that separates,
> and he shall sever the bonds that lash the burden of
> my people, for the True Son is the knife.

Well, Yens *was* born under the day sign Knife, but there were only twenty day signs and everyone had to be born under one of them. There were plenty of other people born on Knife. And Taemon thought about something Da had told him and Yens long ago, when they were first learning scripture: in ancient texts, "he" or "man" or "son" was used to refer to men *or* women. The True Son could actually be a True Daughter, for all anyone knew.

Taemon turned to another passage:

> He shall be born in the lineage of Nathan and shall
> bear the people into the next Sacred Cycle.

Yens *was* a descendant of Nathan. But so was Mam, and her father before her, and back and back. There had to have been another Knife in there somewhere. What made the high priest so sure that the True Son was born *now*, in Yens's time?

He scanned down to the part of the verse that talked about the New Cycle.

> A cycle of peace. A cycle of knowledge. A cycle of
> deliverance. A cycle of new power. And the people shall
> be astounded by the great sign which shall begin the
> next age. Then shall the True Son enter the New Cycle
> through the North Gate.

Interesting, but not very helpful. Da was right. There was no mention of when all this would happen. Which meant the high priest could decide when he wanted it to happen. And who he wanted it to be.

It is for the Heart of the Earth to choose the True Son.

Earth and Sky! That voice was in his head again. The one from after the accident, with Yens. This was dangerous. He had to get rid of it!

Don't talk to me, he thought as forcefully as he could.

The Son who is worthy.

I'm not listening.

The Son who will do what is needful.

"It's my head, and I said get out!" He spoke out loud this time.

Be it so. An impression of amusement flitted across his thoughts, and he felt the voice withdraw.

"And stay out!" Taemon added for good measure.

A few days later, Taemon raced home after school. No psi meant no lunch. He was starving. He dashed up the stairs to the refrigerator in his room, flipped the hidden latch he'd installed, and pulled out bread, a cheese bar, and some ginger water. He wolfed it down.

"Slow down, Taemon. What's the rush?" Mam stood in the doorway, her eyes turned away. She hated to see him eating with his hands.

"Goin' to Moke's house." Taemon swallowed. "Psiball practice."

Mam nodded. "I've been thinking about psiball, and you're right. It's important to keep up appearances. Your father . . . feels differently. But let me talk to him."

Keeping up appearances. Was that the only reason to play psiball? To Taemon it was something more, something to do with what Moke said about dealing with weakness. Something about living his own life. The words were hard to find, so he didn't try. "Thanks, Mam."

"But Taemon, you have to be so careful. One slip and . . ." She sniffed and her mouth quivered. She smiled sadly.

"I know, Mam. Believe me, I know."

She exhaled, relaxed her shoulders, steadied her voice. "Keep practicing. But no tournaments until Da agrees."

"Deal." Taemon finished the last of the cheese and wiped his mouth with the back of his hand.

Mam grimaced.

"Oh . . . sorry." Taemon used his shirtsleeve to wipe his mouth this time. He raced downstairs, out the door, and jogged the six blocks to Moke's.

When he got there, he saw the psiball stuck in the

tree by the side of the house. Good. That was their signal that the practice session was on. At school that day, Moke hadn't been sure if he'd have time to practice this afternoon, said his parents might need help at the crematorium. Taemon didn't want to know what chores might need doing at the place where bodies were cremated. It gave him the tremblies.

The gate in the backyard fence wasn't locked, so Taemon let himself in. "Moke?"

Only the birds called out in response.

"Anyone?" Taemon walked over to the half-sphere and sat on the edge. All that hurrying and Moke wasn't even here.

He waited a few minutes. Was Moke coming or not? Maybe he had to work after all. Would've been nice if he'd remembered to take the ball out of the tree. Taemon decided to walk the five blocks to the crematorium. He could wait there just as easily as he could wait here. And at least he could find out whether the practice was on or off.

The crematorium was an odd building. It looked something like a church in the front, with its stained-glass windows and wooden double doors. But it was boxy and squat, with none of the height and grandeur of a church. And it had chimneys in the back.

The front door was ajar. Taemon leaned forward without looking in. "Hello? Moke?"

Faint voices came from inside. Taemon forced himself to look. He'd never been inside, and he wasn't sure what to expect. The front room looked well lit. Padded chairs lined the perimeter of the room, and paintings in pastel colors hung on the walls. It didn't look so bad. Taemon ventured in.

"Moke?" He didn't think he should yell, so he tried as loud a whisper as he could manage. "Hoy, Moke!"

He heard voices again. Was it Moke? He took a few tentative steps down the hallway on the left.

". . . due to the uniqueness of the situation." That sounded like Elder Naseph. What was he doing here?

"Our family has been running the crematorium for generations. This is clearly outside regulations." The second voice belonged to Moke's father.

"The high priest requires it. You need no further explanation."

"So you'll be taking both of these cadavers to the temple?"

Cadavers as in bodies? Bodies as in dead? Taemon shuddered. Dead bodies had to be the most taboo thing in Deliverance. For good reason. Besides healers and midwives, no one was allowed to know what the inside of the body looked like. It was too much knowledge for a psi wielder. If you knew how the body worked, you might try using psi on the inside of the body. You could hurt someone like that—someone like your brother, who made you so mad you couldn't stand it anymore.

The front door clicked. Someone was in the waiting room. He'd rather not be caught eavesdropping. The voices came from a room on his left, so Taemon leaned on the nearest door to the right. It was locked.

"There you are!" Taemon nearly jumped through the roof, but it was only Moke who came from the waiting room.

"Don't scare me like that."

Moke grinned. "A little jittery your first time in the crematorium? Can't imagine why."

The voice from the room grew louder. "We will discuss this no further. The decision is made."

With a questioning look, Moke turned to Taemon and mouthed, "Who?"

"Naseph," Taemon whispered.

"We'd better get out of here," Moke whispered back. Taemon could not agree more. He was about to turn toward the front room when Moke used psi to open the door Taemon had been leaning against. They both stumbled into a dark, cool room.

"We'll wait here until they leave."

"Is it safe?" Taemon asked.

Moke chuckled. "Yeah. Nobody's allowed in here. This is where we keep the cadavers until the healers' guild picks them up."

The answer sent chills across Taemon's skin. "They were talking about taking cadavers to the temple."

"What? That can't be right," Moke whispered. "Only healers are allowed to have cadavers. You know, to train new healers."

"Your da seemed pretty upset," Taemon said. "What would the high priest want with—?"

Before he could finish the sentence, the door opened. Moke's father and Elder Naseph stood in the doorway.

8 RAIN

Rain storms in, and Stone must yield—
Rain, the friend to flow'r and field.
He nurtures grain and opens bud,
But too much rain will cause a flood.
By show'r or flood, the Earth is healed.
By show'r or flood, the Earth is healed.

— CALENDAR SONG

Elder Naseph's face hardened. "What sacrilege is this? Boys allowed to view cadavers?"

Taemon looked over his shoulder. Light from the hallway spilled into the room and revealed two white sheets that covered whatever was lying on the tables. It wasn't hard to figure out what was under the sheets, but Taemon refused to name it in his mind.

Moke's da shook his head and used psi to pull the boys into the hall. "This is my son and his friend. They are *not* allowed in there."

"Yet there they were. Do you understand how vital this is, Brother Daveen?" Elder Naseph's face was red. The cords in his neck stood out. He was shaking enough to jingle his beard trinkets. "No one can have access to cadavers. This community's safety depends on protecting the sacredness of the human body. If you can't safeguard these bodies, someone else will take your place."

Moke's father bowed his head. "I understand. I'll be more careful."

Taemon and Moke tried to slink down the hallway, but Elder Naseph yanked them backward with psi. Taemon felt his chin being pressed upward, forcing him to look at the incensed priest.

Elder Naseph turned to Moke first. "You I can overlook. After all, you will work here someday. But you!" Now the priest trained his angry glare on Taemon. "You could go to the asylum for this. Have you been there? Seen what the serum does?"

Taemon shook his head. The serum was a drug that caused disorientation and delirium. It was given to dangerous criminals to make them unable to focus, unable to use psi.

Taemon felt his collar tighten around his neck as the priest continued. "It's not pleasant, I assure you. We're watching you, boy. You are this close to experiencing the serum firsthand." He held his manicured, bejeweled fingers in front of Taemon's face.

Taemon tried to nod, but the upward pressure on his chin allowed little more than a tiny bob. Maybe the elders didn't know he was powerless after all. Otherwise, why would Elder Naseph threaten him with the serum? If there was anyone who didn't need the serum, it was Taemon.

As soon as he felt the priest's psi withdraw, Taemon ran out the front door with Moke. They didn't stop running until they reached Moke's backyard, where they collapsed on the grass.

Moke's panting turned into laughter. "Did you see his face? I didn't know nostrils could flare that wide."

"He was mad, all right," Taemon said. They were watching him. How? Were people spying on him? His teachers? His neighbors? Moke? Skies, he hoped it wasn't Moke. His stomach turned at the thought. All these plots and secrets and suspicions. When had life gotten so complicated?

Moke imitated the priest's nasaly voice: "'It'll be the serum for you!' It was like he was scared of something."

"I don't know what *he* has to be afraid of," Taemon said. "But you can bet I'm never going back to that place again."

"Everybody goes to the crematorium eventually," Moke said darkly. "What I want to know is why does the high priest want cadavers all of a sudden? It must be connected to training the True Son. Have you heard anything about Yens?"

Taemon shook his head. "Nothing for sure. We're not allowed to talk to him, though Uncle Fierre saw him with the priests and a group of seven or eight other kids. No one we knew." The True Son was the only thing anyone wanted to talk about. Rumors were flying, and Taemon didn't know what to believe.

Moke puffed up his chest. "Then maybe I still have a chance. I always thought he should pick me."

Taemon laughed and felt his tension ease. "Cha, right."

He could trust Moke. He had to.

In the Sacred Cycle, Rain was a symbol of prosperity. It was prospering cats and dogs at the moment. Today was the Sabbath, and Taemon was going to church with his parents to bring an offering. Would the priests reveal what was going on at the temple? What would they say?

When Taemon came downstairs, he saw Da carrying the offering box with his bare hands. Homegrown tomatoes, squash, peppers, and three generous measures of grain filled the box. He lugged it into the living room, set it by the door, stood up, and rubbed his back. "Feels good to do things without psi once in a while. Builds character, builds muscle, helps you remember that psi is a gift from the Heart of the Earth."

This was Da's weekly speech about keeping the Sabbath. It used to be unlawful to use psi on the Sabbath day. But life without psi—even if just for a day—was inconvenient, difficult even, so everyone basically ignored that rule. Everyone except Da. His archaic Sabbath observance had always been a little embarrassing, but now it was the one bright day in each of Taemon's dreary weeks, a short rest from the hard work of keeping up appearances.

I don't need that speech anymore, thought Taemon. *I do without psi every day.* But he didn't say it. Mam and Da were anxious this morning, and he had no wish to make it worse.

"I can carry it if you want," Taemon said.

"Go ahead," Da said. "Take a turn. This is how my father took his offering to church, and my grandfather before that. See the worn handles on the box? That represents the Houser family's tradition of devotion." Da's voice held the same passion, the same resolve, even under the pressure from the elders. Taemon had to wonder if Da was acting brave or foolish.

Into the room walked Mam, who used psi to place her embroidered tablecloth on top of the vegetables, then arrange it just so. Then she turned to inspect Taemon.

"Wiljamen." She spoke to Da but didn't look at him. Instead she was using psi to smooth Taemon's jacket and straighten his cuffs. "You're not going to make a fuss today, are you? Remember what's at stake."

"I'll be fine," Da said. "Let's go."

Taemon picked up the offering box and followed his parents out the door. They would walk to church, just as they did every week, since Da would never agree to drive the quadrider on the Sabbath. That would require psi. Good thing it wasn't far.

Fat rain pelted Taemon as soon as he stepped off the porch. The box was heavy, and he felt clumsy with it.

"Don't drop it," Da said.

"I won't." Taemon tried to find a better position for the box.

Mam fumbled with an umbrella, an absurd mushroom-shaped thing with a handle. No one used umbrellas anymore. She attempted to cover Taemon and the offering box while she and Da got half-soaked in the rain.

Taemon noticed the strange looks from people passing by in their quadriders. They made an odd sight, the three of them lurching and stumbling down the sidewalk, awkwardly trying to stay together under an umbrella that couldn't possibly cover them all.

At church, the sanctuary was buzzing with talk. Taemon couldn't hear the words, but he was certain it was about the True Son.

Taemon was the only one who walked up and carried the box to the front of the sanctuary and placed the offerings on the table one by one. Everyone else used psi. He looked at the other offerings on the table. Gold and silver items were popular — cups, platters, jewelry, garden decorations. Glassware, beautifully crafted. Expensive spices. Quite a bit of clothing this Sabbath, in bright colors, elaborately fashioned and embroidered. There was a telescope that looked interesting. The vegetables and grain from Taemon's family were among the few edible items. He returned to his seat.

Da was frowning, and Taemon knew why. Seemed like every Sabbath the offerings included less food and more trinkets. The offerings were supposed to help the poor people and also support the priests. Of course the priests were the ones who decided who got what, and Taemon was pretty sure that silver tray with the gold filigree edge wasn't going to end up on a poor family's table. Most of the finery went to the priests while the poor people got poorer. It didn't sit well with Da.

Sure enough, Taemon heard Da whisper, "Poor people need tomatoes more than they need earrings."

Mam glared at him.

When the singing began, Taemon felt himself relax. Hearing Da's deep, rich voice soothed his thoughts.

The hymn ended, and the priest walked in. Only it wasn't the priest who normally officiated at Taemon's church. It was the high priest himself, Elder Naseph, who walked to the pulpit in all his finery and his jinglery. Taemon wondered if he used psi to make them jangle more noisily. Following the high priest were the innocents, the powerless people who lived in the temple and served the priests. Taemon had always ignored them before, but lately he'd been studying them when he could. Was there any way to tell they were powerless? Did it show in their faces? In their bearing? It was hard to say. The innocents kept their heads bowed and their eyes downcast.

Elder Naseph reached the pulpit, and the innocents took their places behind him. The huge book of scripture resting on the pulpit opened itself.

Da opened his book also. Da didn't use psi, this being the Sabbath and all, so he held the book with his hands and turned the pages with his fingers. The pages rustled noisily. Done with psi, it would have been silent. People glared at him, including Mam, but Da acted like he didn't notice.

A silent exchange took place between Elder Naseph and Da. The high priest's intimidating glower seemed to have no effect on Da. He returned the glower with a steady, serene look, as if he'd done nothing wrong. Which he'd hadn't. Not really.

Elder Naseph broke the staring duel when he looked down to read from the scriptures. "'The Son who is True shall bear the people into the next Sacred Cycle. A cycle of knowledge. A cycle of new power. A cycle of leadership over many nations.'"

What was that? Taemon had just read that passage a few days ago, and he was sure it didn't say those things. Where was the part about peace and deliverance? Without turning his head, Taemon shifted his gaze to Da's book and followed the passage. Sure enough, it was just as Taemon had remembered it. Elder Naseph had changed it. He knew Da was reading along. Was he openly taunting Da? Daring him to object?

The scriptures on the pulpit closed, and Elder Naseph looked over the congregation. "The great day is at hand. You shall tell your children and your grandchildren that you saw the beginning of the Sacred Cycle of Power. It is time for the people gifted by the Heart of the Earth to lead the world in righteousness."

The high priest paused to let his words weave their spell. Taemon wondered what "lead the world" meant. Was he talking about ending the hundreds of years of isolation from the powerless world? That couldn't be right. When the first of Nathan's descendants had tried to live in the nonpsi world, it had led to nothing but paranoia and hatred during the Great War. The idea alone made Taemon feel queasy.

He turned to look at Da. His father's face was as still as concrete.

Elder Naseph continued. "Great blessings do not come without great sacrifice. You will be asked to contribute your psi to the community in ways that have not been asked before. There is no room for doubt. There is no place for questioning. Only through exact obedience will the new cycle of power take place."

Taemon looked around the sanctuary. Were people believing this? Were they that blind? He studied the faces that surrounded him. Eager. Excited. Enthralled.

"Prepare yourselves and your families. For on the day One Quake, the True Son will be announced and the Cycle of Power shall begin."

Taemon frowned. One Quake was his birthday, a couple months away. He would be thirteen.

9 BEETLE

Rain dries out; its day is through,

For Beetle has so much to do.

While diligence is much admired,

Drudgery is not required.

It all lies in your point of view.

It all lies in your point of view.

— CALENDAR SONG

Everyone in Deliverance was obsessed with the announcement of the True Son. It was weeks away, but everyone had a prediction about who would be chosen, about what astonishing thing would be done. Huge parties were in the planning for the night of the ceremony, and getting invited to the right party was crucial.

But Taemon had more important things on his mind. Things like how to get by without being able to open doors with psi. Or staying after school to finish a project because he couldn't take it home without carrying it by hand. Or learning how to play a musical instrument without psi.

Music was a required class because it developed discipline and precision with psi. Da had arranged to get Taemon excused from music class until he recovered completely from his accident, but Brother Usaro's patience had long ago run out, and it was time for Taemon to come up with a new plan. First, he convinced Brother Usaro to let him switch to the bass drum. He told the teacher he needed lots of extra practice and asked permission to take the drum home for the weekend. Da had to carry it home for him.

In Da's workshop, Taemon took the drum apart. Knowing that drums used to be played with sticks and mallets in the days before psi, he tinkered with different contraptions until he figured out how to rig a mallet attached to a lever inside the drum. On the outside of the drum, disguised among the tension rods and mounting lugs, he added a bar that he could push with his foot or knee to control the mallet. He put it all back together and even managed to tune it properly.

He practiced for hours in the workshop, different

positions, different ways to use the lever without drawing attention to it. Now it was time to join the music class.

Unfortunately, they were working on a particularly difficult piece at the moment.

"Not bad," Brother Usaro said after the first run-through.

Not bad? The orchestra had the musical quality of a quadrider crash.

"We have to sort a few things out," Brother Usaro said. "Try that again while I listen for trouble spots." He used psi to start his baton bouncing the rhythm at the front of the room. Meanwhile, he walked around the classroom, weaving between the students, tilting his head and listening intently.

As the teacher made his way to the back of the room, Taemon found it more difficult to concentrate. He couldn't seem to stay with the beat.

Brother Usaro stopped next to Taemon and waited for the end of the song.

Taemon wanted to groan.

"The foundation for every orchestra is the percussion. We'll start with the bass drum."

Why had he thought this could work? His plan was unraveling on the very first day of music class!

Brother Usaro stood right behind him. "Lay down a steady beat for us, Taemon."

The drum was on its stand. Taemon stood next to it and casually rested his thumb on the lever. He played, keeping his body as still as possible like all musicians did. The idea was that movement or facial expressions might distract from the music itself. Taemon had to move his thumb a squinch, but he positioned his body to shield the movement from the teacher's view.

Brother Usaro rubbed his chin. "Hmm. Something's not right. Let me try."

Taemon held his breath as Brother Usaro played the drum himself.

"Seems okay," he muttered. "Let's hear you play one more time."

Again Taemon assumed his casual position, which he had rehearsed carefully at home, moved his thumb in place, and played the drum.

"Aha! I see what you're doing."

Taemon flinched and prepared for the worst.

"You are mistakenly applying psi to the inside of the

drum and pushing it outward," Brother Usaro said. "It's a subtle difference, but I can see it now. I want you to use your psi to push on the outside of the drum. Push it inward, not outward. Try again."

Skies! How was he supposed to push inward? The mallet only worked one way. Taemon took his position and played the drum the only way he could, which was exactly the same way he had played it a moment ago.

"No, that's still not right," Brother Usaro said.

Taemon bit his lip and screwed up his face, hoping to imitate utmost concentration. "I'll get it this time."

He played again. The same way.

Brother Usaro frowned.

The class murmured, and Taemon heard them shifting in their seats. He looked at Brother Usaro and shrugged. "I guess I've been practicing the wrong way all this time. It might take me a while to change."

Brother Usaro nodded. "Keep trying. You'll get it." He moved on to the other percussionists.

Taemon closed his eyes and sent a silent prayer of gratitude to the Heart of the Earth.

• • •

Uff! The psiball hit Taemon in the stomach. He and Moke had been practicing psiball for two hours in Moke's backyard.

"Perfect!" Moke yelled. "That's exactly what we need. If you block the ball with your body, it doesn't matter how much psi the other team has. Let's do it again."

"This time I'll throw the ball and you do the *uff*," Taemon said.

Moke laughed. "You'll never get an *uff* out of me."

After weeks of practice, their strategies were finally coming together. When the ball got past Moke and rolled into the weeds, they decided to call it quits for the day. Then, as had become their custom, they collapsed on the grass to discuss strategy.

"Here's what I think we should to do," Moke said. "If we get to a point in the game where we need to move the ball with psi—I'm not talking about a lot, just a squinch— then I say we use it."

Taemon watched a beetle crawl over his shoe. "I thought the whole point was not using psi. I mean, not for ball handling anyway."

Moke shrugged. "All I'm saying is, if it comes down to

winning the game or not, I'm not above using a tiny bit of psi to move the ball."

"I guess you're right."

"You bet your sweet binky I'm right." Moke said. "We have to win at least one game this weekend."

"This weekend?" Taemon sat up.

"Cha. The tournament. I signed us up."

"Skies! I told you I can't do tournaments. My parents won't let me."

"Oops!" Moke said. "My mistake. Guess that slipped my mind." His sly grin was anything but apologetic. "Come on, brother, where's your sense of social responsibility? Don't you want to show everybody that weak freaks are not thoroughly worthless?"

"I can't." *I can't.* The words echoed inside Taemon's head. If Moke only knew how true those two words really were. "Look, Moke, my parents are really upset. Can you blame them? The priests are not allowing any contact with Yens. All these rumors are flying around. Know what I heard yesterday? That they're teaching the True Son recruits to raise the dead."

"That's stupid," Moke said. "Those people don't know what they're talking about."

"Yeah, but how do you think it makes my parents feel? They're distracted and tense, and I can't push them with this tournament thing right now."

"Okay, well, maybe they don't have to know about it," Moke said.

Taemon shook his head. "Can't. Sorry. Gotta go." He got up and walked away before Moke could press any further.

The next day, music class was much the same. Brother Usaro tried different ways to help Taemon visualize playing the drum the right way. Taemon pretended to try and continually apologized for his mistakes. It was becoming a real pain in the hinderpart.

After a particularly dreadful performance, Brother Usaro sighed. "Taemon, see me after class."

He was not looking forward to another one of Brother Usaro's pep talks. He knew it by heart by now: *Feel the music. Relax. Anxiety is your enemy.*

Taemon resolved to take the drum home for additional experimentation. He could get Da to carry it home for him. Maybe he could figure out a better system for invisible psiless drum playing. All this worry made Taemon lose his place several times before music class was finally over. He trudged into Brother Usaro's office.

"You're still playing the drum wrong," the teacher said.

Taemon nodded. "I'm trying, I really am. I'll figure it out one of these days."

"Once we get into marching band, you're going to have to move that bass drum while you play it. That's the biggest instrument we've got. It's not easy to move."

Marching band next year. He had no idea how he was going to solve that problem. Of course no one actually marched anymore. That term came from pre-psi days. Now the musicians stood along the edge of the room and moved the instruments in interesting patterns and arrangements as they played.

"I want you to try something else," said Brother Usaro. "A different instrument."

Panic welled up inside Taemon. He shook his head. "No, thank you, sir. My da says never give up. And changing instruments feels like giving up. I'm just . . . I'm slow."

"What about going back to a wind instrument? You were showing some promise before the accid—" Brother

Usaro cleared his throat. "You showed promise in my class last year."

How under the blazing sun would he manage a wind instrument? Taemon pictured the trumpet, the flute, the saxophone. They all required psi to force air into the instrument.

"Just think about it," Brother Usaro said. "That's all I ask."

Taemon exhaled. "I'll definitely be thinking about it."

Things weren't much easier at home. His parents were edgy. He knew they were worried about Yens. There wasn't much anyone could do but wait until the announcement and see what happened. Taemon also knew they were worried about his situation. He wished they'd stop fretting about every little thing.

"Put those socks in the hamper," Mam said as she walked past the open door of the bathroom.

Taemon reached down to pick up his socks.

"Not with your hands!" Mam's voice was sharp. "Earth and Sky, do you want someone to see that?" The socks flew into the hamper with Mam's psi. "Besides, they're filthy. I don't want you touching them."

How else was he supposed to pick things up? Taemon wanted to scream. Sometimes it was like she forgot he was powerless. He managed to control his tone. "We're standing in the bathroom. Who's going to see?"

"Me! I see. Every time I see you using your hands, it reminds me . . ." She sniffed, swallowed hard, and walked away.

She was upset. He understood that. He should try harder to be patient.

Da came in. "She's trying to protect you, son. We've come up with a plan. We'll work together to keep you safe and get you through the rest of this school year. After that, we can get you into an early apprenticeship. You'll be my teaching apprentice at school, and we'll cover things up until you get your psi back."

So, no marching band next year after all. That could work. Taemon always knew he'd be his father's apprentice someday; he just hadn't expected it to happen so soon. Boys followed in their families' vocations. Girls waited until after they got married to train for the vocation of their husband's family. That's just how it was. Otherwise, too many people would know how to do things they had no business doing. Thirteen was the very soonest a person could become an apprentice, but most people chose to continue in school until they were at least seventeen. Only weaklings quit school early. *That's me,* thought Taemon.

"Da, you need to understand something. I'm not going to get my psi back. It's gone."

Da let out a soft sigh. "Son, sometimes during adolescence, a young man's body is changing and . . ."

Ugh. Not the-goose-and-the-gander talk. Losing his psi had nothing to do with raging hormones. Taemon closed his eyes, breathed deeply, and tried to push his frustration aside. "No, Da. It's not that."

"Well, what then? Where do you envision your life going? You can't make decisions right now, Taemon. You've got to be patient until—"

"Until nothing," Taemon said. "I *can* make decisions. I'm handling this. I handle it every day. I can do things, Da. I'm powerless, but I'm not stupid."

"Lower your voice," Da said sternly.

I'll do better than that, Taemon thought. *I'll end this conversation.* He stared resolutely at Da, then pushed past him and left the room. Taemon's shoulder shoved against his father's arm. It was a small shove, but it got the point across.

The psiball tournament might not be such a bad idea after all.

10 EAGLE

As Beetle's day sets in the west,

Eagle soars above the rest,

Circling, wheeling overhead.

Achievement is by struggle bred.

Success can lead to loneliness.

Success can lead to loneliness.

— CALENDAR SONG

Only a few seconds were left in the game. Four psiball players stood inside one huge sphere, two teams of two. They were sweaty, spent, and tense. Taemon and Moke were ahead, but not by much. If the other team scored, they'd win.

The sphere was made of lead crystal — smooth, sturdy, and perfectly transparent so that spectators could watch the game.

The other team had possession of the ball. Taemon watched the girl's eyes, looking for any indication of which way she would send the heavy leather ball. Blocking the hole wasn't permitted, but blocking wasn't what Taemon had in mind.

The whole idea of psiball was to use psi to direct the ball toward the hole, turn the hole your team's color, and send the ball through. The side holes were worth one point, the top hole worth three.

Each team tried to send their psi more forcefully and more quickly to the ball. The ball would obey the psi order that was received first, or in some cases, the psi order that carried more authority. Players sometimes moved around the sphere, since field of vision and proximity to the ball might lend advantage, but these movements were not critical to the game. Players preferred to spend their energy on psi rather than muscle. Strong psi, quick psi, controlled psi—that's what won psiball games.

Until Moke and Taemon came along.

They ran. They spun. They jumped. They did somersaults and backflips and handstands. Anything to make it difficult for the opposite team to mentally project a path to one of the holes. For Taemon and Moke, it was all about defense, aggressive and confusing defense. No one had seen anything like it.

Of course Taemon and Moke did have to score at least a few points. Now and then they managed to gain possession of the ball and kick it or roll it into a hole. Physical contact with the ball was not illegal unless it lasted more than three seconds. Most players avoided physical contact because it was so tiring. The ball was heavy, and it didn't bounce. But weeks of practice had made Taemon's and Moke's bodies strong and agile.

This was their closest game so far. This team was good, very good. Taemon waited, alert and eager, watching for their opponents' next move. He saw that one of the side holes had turned orange, which usually meant that's where the ball was headed. But it could be a trick. Taemon thought he saw the other player flash a glance toward the top hole.

Taemon smiled. *Where you look is where you go.* He saw where the player had looked; now he knew where the ball would go.

The ball careened in a jagged path, heading for the orange hole on the side. But Taemon decided to defend the top hole instead. He didn't have time to think anymore. He had to move. Now.

He took a couple of running steps up the slope of the

sphere, jumped, and flipped. He planted both palms on the floor of the sphere and pushed upward with everything he had. He needed as much height as possible. At this point, he couldn't see the ball. All he could do was stretch his legs up, kick wildly, and hope he'd guessed right.

He thought he felt something glance off his heel. Either he'd made contact with the ball or he'd kicked Moke in the head. Flipping his legs under his body again, Taemon landed and rolled with the momentum so he wouldn't break any bones.

The buzzer sounded. The ball rested inside the bottom of the sphere. No goal.

The crowd responded with gasps and oohs. Not exactly applause, more like astonishment. It didn't matter. Taemon knew his acrobatics had made an impression.

Moke hugged him. "We did it!"

"Victory awarded to the Blue Team," the announcer said. The top of the sphere lifted up, and all four players climbed out.

The boy and girl from the opposing team immediately ran to the umpire. "That was hole tending!" the girl said.

"His foot did not linger in front of the hole," said the umpire. "It's bizarre, but it's not illegal."

The boy glared at Taemon. "This is not psiball. This is pathetic."

Taemon turned away. Moke was using psi to squirt water over Taemon's head from the drinking flask. Taemon laughed and shook his head, spattering the water in Moke's face.

They needed to rest. In only a couple of hours, they'd play in the championship match for their age group. He followed Moke into the locker room.

"Brother, you sweat like a sow," Moke said. "You'd better take a shower before the next match."

Taemon had to think quickly. He couldn't turn on the water, not without psi, but he couldn't let Moke see that. These moments happened many times each day, and Taemon had come to pride himself on finding creative ways to avoid certain situations.

"Nah," Taemon said. "Stink works in our favor, remember? Distracts the other team."

Moke laughed. "I'm *not* climbing inside a psiball sphere with you and your reek. You gotta shower."

"Fine, but I gotta pee first. You go ahead, take your shower. And leave the water on for me, cha?"

"Cha indeed," Moke said, heading for the shower.

Taking his full water flask with him, Taemon went into the toilet stall. He didn't need to pee. What he really needed was a drink. He couldn't let anyone see him holding the water flask while he drank. In the privacy of the stall, he gulped down the water.

He thought about the games they'd played at the tournament today. Five so far, with one more to go. All their strategies worked perfectly, just like they'd practiced. It felt good to win, to be skilled at something. It felt good to be clever, unique, impressive. It felt really good.

Moke had been right. Taemon needed this tournament to prove to himself that his intelligence and physical strength could make up for his lack of psi. Being psiless was not the same as being powerless. For the first time, he felt there was nothing he couldn't do, no one he couldn't fool.

He wasn't even afraid of facing Mam and Da tonight and telling them about the tournament. Da would not be pleased, but if Yens could get away with being a psiball champion, Taemon could, too.

• • •

Showered, hydrated, and rested, Taemon was ready for the final game. He and Moke joked while they stretched and warmed up.

As they walked out to the sphere, Taemon saw the Eagle trophy, golden and glittering, resting on a table in front of the sphere. The winning team would take it home. He imagined it sitting in his living room, next to Yens's many trophies. Eagle, the sign for achievement. Maybe this would finally convince Da that Taemon could make his own way in this world.

A smattering of hisses came from the audience. So they were not the darlings of tournament, so what? Nothing could bring Taemon down. This was his day. His and Moke's and all the other freaklings' out there.

The umpire motioned for the players to enter the sphere. The hostility showed clearly in the two boys on the Red Team. Their jaws were clenched, their gazes cold. Even their customary pregame nods had a certain menace in them.

Taemon gave a curt nod. *Let's just get on with it,* he thought.

The umpire climbed out of the sphere and lowered the top half, enclosing the players inside. The buzzer sounded, and the game began.

The game was crazy from the first second. These players had obviously been watching Taemon and Moke. They were using many of the same physical techniques to defend the holes. They weren't very practiced or polished, but they had the right idea. At the end of the first quarter, the other team had a sizable lead. During the next two quarters, Taemon and Moke managed to cut down that lead, but they were still behind by three points.

During the break before the last quarter, Taemon could hardly catch his breath.

"These guys," said Moke. "So aggressive. I wouldn't be surprised if they're both born Jaguars."

"Cha," Taemon said, panting. "They got our number."

"We've gotta stir things up, get them off balance," Moke said.

"Cha."

"Here's my idea," Moke began, but the warning buzzer cut him off. Time to get back into the sphere. "Just follow my lead."

The frenetic pace of the game resumed when the

buzzer sounded. The ball hurled in erratic patterns inside the sphere. Players hopped, twisted, kicked, and dove—anything to keep the ball away from the holes.

Taemon found it more and more difficult to stay focused. In an unguarded moment, he lost track of the ball. Before he could get his bearings, it came rushing toward him, smacked him square in the stomach, and knocked his breath out. He clutched the ball and leaned over.

For a moment, he was stunned. He couldn't inhale. He opened his mouth, but no air would go inside.

"Foul!" Moke yelled. "Rough play! That was intentional."

But the umpire hadn't made the call. The game was still in play, and Taemon was still holding the ball.

Moke called for a time-out and at the very same instant, the umpire called a foul on Taemon.

"Holding!" screamed the two Red players.

"Rough play!" screamed Moke. "That was dirty, and you know it!"

"Dirty?" yelled one of the players. "You want dirty?" He leaped on Moke and started punching.

Taemon was still trying to catch his breath.

The other Red player jumped Moke, too. Horrified

gasps came from the audience, many of whom had likely never witnessed such violent physical contact before. The three boys fought while the umpire lifted the top off the sphere. By the time they were pried apart by psi, each boy had smears of blood on his face. The three were ordered out of the sphere while the two umpires conferred.

Taemon was finally able to take a breath. He pulled air into his chest in big shuddering gasps.

The referee stepped up to the sphere. "Penalty shot awarded to Blue Team. First Red Player ejected for five seconds. Second Red Player ejected for five seconds."

Moke whooped. Taemon smiled. They could easily score in five seconds without the opposing team in the sphere. Physical contact wasn't allowed for penalty shots, but Moke could use a little psi. He wouldn't even have to color the hole since it was a penalty shot and the other team wasn't in the sphere. It would be an easy score, even for a weak freak.

But the referee hadn't finished. "First Blue Player ejected for five seconds."

It took Taemon a few seconds to realize what had happened. Everyone had been ejected but him. He was the one who would take the penalty shot.

"That's okay," Moke said. "You can do it. Remember what we said? Just a squinch."

Taemon was stunned. His mind went blank. He looked around at the crowd of spectators, then chided himself. What help did he expect? What could he do? Who could get him out of this?

None.

Nothing.

No one.

The top of the crystal sphere lowered with Taemon alone inside. The ball sat motionless at the bottom of the sphere, only a couple of feet from the nearest hole.

No tricks could save him. No magnets, no sleight of hand, no clever distraction.

"So easy a baby could do it," one of the Red players said.

The buzzer sounded to begin the penalty shot.

Taemon stared at the ball. Each second that ticked off the clock seemed like an aeon.

The crowd yelled.

Moke cheered.

Taemon could do nothing.

"Five!" the crowd chanted. "Four! Three!"

The tournament had been a mistake. *Better to stay out of the psiball leagues altogether.*

"Two!"

Da was right. *You can't make decisions, Taemon.*

"One!"

The buzzer sounded.

The crowd gradually grew silent. Then the murmurs started.

"Is he powerless?"

"Disabled?"

"Feebleminded?"

"No psi at all?"

Moke ran up and placed his palms on the sphere, his face filled with shock.

Taemon stared at him. "I can't."

PART TWO

11 KNIFE

As Eagle flies beyond the curve,
Knife cuts in with steely nerve.
Sharp and eager, clean, decisive,
Knife is keen to be divisive.
A Knife may injure or may serve.
A Knife may injure or may serve.

— CALENDAR SONG

Taemon walked through the greenhouse, looking for anything that was ripe. With a gloved hand, he moved a broad
leaf aside and found a bumpy yellow squash. He twisted
the gourd off the vine and dropped it into the cloth sack
slung over his shoulder. Continuing his search, he peeked
under squash leaves, checked the color of peppers, judged
the size of cabbages.

He stared at the gloves on his hands. He'd never even
seen gloves until he came to the powerless colony a
month ago. In the city, anything dirty or rough was done

with psi. Now he lived with a family who'd taken him in. He worked at a farm and wore gloves. Everything was different here—knobs on the doors, buttons on clothes, handles on everything, bizarre gadgets like scissors required to complete the simplest of tasks.

Taemon pulled a knife from his tool belt and used it to remove a cabbage from its stem. A knife! He never thought he'd see one, much less hold one. He remembered Mam singing the calendar song to him every night when he was small. Most of the day signs were animals and things from nature, things he'd seen before. But he had to ask Mam what a knife was. Now he remembered her answer: a savage tool used to separate one thing from another.

What would Mam and Da think of their savage son?

Mam. Da. The last time he saw them was at the authority station. One of the referees at the tournament had escorted him there after the terrible moment when he'd revealed his secret. The authority officers had locked him in a holding cell and sent a runner to get his parents. Mam had come in first, pale and trembling. Taemon couldn't remember exactly what he'd said, but it involved several repetitions of "I'm sorry." Mam, however, never said a word. She looked so shaken, Taemon wondered if she even understood what was happening.

Then Mam left and they let Da come in. Da, who blustered and argued with the guards, preaching tolerance and compassion. *Let it go, Da,* Taemon had wanted to say. *I can't stay here. I don't deserve to stay here. Let them take me.*

And in the end, of course, Da had no choice but to do just that.

Would he ever see his parents again? Powerless people were not allowed in the city any more than psiwielders were allowed in the colony. There was no reason for them to mingle. Psiwielders saw powerless people as worthless, and powerless people, he'd quickly realized, saw psiwielders as treacherous. With the religious exception of the innocents in the temple, the two groups had long ago agreed to keep their distance. There was a drop-off station between the two where messages and goods could be exchanged. He'd been hoping for a package from Mam or a letter from Da, but so far, nothing. Then again, in a city where people didn't write anymore, letters would seem suspicious, like Da was planning something. Maybe his da was finally learning to keep quiet and stay out of trouble.

"Need any help?"

Taemon turned. It was Hannova, the leader of the colony.

"I heard you wanted to see me," Taemon said. "Had to finish in the greenhouse first."

"Why don't I help you," said Hannova. "We can work and talk at the same time." Already she was plucking a red tomato from the vine.

Taemon knew what Hannova wanted. He was turning thirteen tomorrow, and in the colony that meant it was time to start learning a trade. That was another big difference between the city and the colony. The only decision a city kid had to make was when to start his apprenticeship. Thirteen was the earliest age, but a person could keep going to school until age seventeen if he or she chose. As far as choosing your occupation, that just didn't happen. Trade secrets were jealously kept within families. Children followed their family's occupation. If Taemon had stayed in the city, he would have been a teacher, like Da. Exceptions were made only when a child showed exceptional talent in music, art, or sports—which was why Yens put so much effort into psiball. If he was good enough, he could play for one of the professional teams instead of being Da's apprentice.

Taemon studied one of the peppers, then left it alone. How was he supposed to tell when a green pepper was ripe? And how was he supposed to know what occupation was right for him? He'd never thought about it before. Colony kids had thirteen years to figure it out. No one knew what to do with a thirteen-year-old who'd only just come from the city.

At least they hadn't made him go to school for the weeks before his birthday. Hannova had decided to let him test out two or three trial apprenticeships before he had to choose. So far, he'd worked at the bakery, the shoemaker's, and the farm, and he still didn't know what he wanted to do. Taemon was sure that's what Hannova wanted to talk about.

"Do you like working at the farm?" Hannova asked.

"S'okay, I guess."

"You can stay here permanently if you want. I know Bynon would love to keep a hard worker like you."

Taemon shrugged.

"I heard you made a new plow."

"The old one was rusted. Falling apart."

"Bynon said you made several improvements in the design."

Taemon reached for another tomato. "Seemed like there might be a better way to do it, that's all. The blacksmith did the hard part."

"Hmm. Are we done here?" Hannova asked.

Taemon nodded. "I think we got everything."

"Let's take a walk. There's someone I'd like you to meet." She patted his back, which startled him. He was still trying to get used to the way people shook hands, held hands, clapped, patted, even hugged. It surprised him how often people communicated through physical touch. Most surprising of all was that he found he actually *liked* it.

After dropping the vegetables off at the farmhouse, Hannova led Taemon to the square at the center of the colony. Today was barter day, and the square was festive with displays of colorful cloth, jams, knitted hats, warm bread, jewelry, herbal remedies, clay pots, hand-carved wooden boxes. Dozens of tables were laid out with peculiar assortments.

A group of musicians played a lively tune with hand-made stringed instruments, a drum, and a flute. The tune was simple, not nearly as complex as the psi music he knew, but he had to admit this music had more emotion, more feeling. The musicians swayed and bounced when they played, their faces showing something that Taemon was sure he'd never experienced. They were the complete opposite of psi musicians, who prided themselves on playing without any motion or facial expression.

The walkways bustled with people wanting to trade and some just wanting to talk. Small children danced and played and laughed while their parents traded. One mother had knelt down, holding her child's chin with one hand while she wiped his tears. She hugged him, then tousled his hair, a combination which seemed to have a calming effect. Taemon found himself wishing his mam had done that for him.

A sharp rapping sound made him wince. He turned and saw someone hanging a sign over one of the booths. Even the sounds were different here. Banging, grinding, creaking, pounding. He'd never realized how noisy primitive life was.

But primitive life had its advantages, too. He could tell who was doing what. Everything felt relaxed and friendly and open. Of course, that relaxed feeling probably had something to do with the fact that he was not required to lie, cheat, or pretend to be anything other than what he was.

Getting through the square took a long time because Hannova greeted each person she saw. She stopped at a table laden with rows of vibrant woven scarves. "This is exquisite," she said, stroking a blue-and-orange wrap of some kind. "Will my sister like it for her birthday?"

"She does," said Challis, the middle-aged woman who sat behind the table. Taemon had already learned to avoid her. She said odd things and always called him by the wrong name.

"Ah, you've come to see your auntie Challis. It was always good to see you, Thayer."

"Um, you too," Taemon said.

Hannova looked confused. "What did she call you?"

Taemon whispered to Hannova, "I think she's got me mixed up with her nephew."

"Thayer's my father, not my nephew. And another thing, the pickles next year were excellent. Sour, just the way I like them."

"Next year?" Taemon asked.

"It's all in the eyebrows, Thayer." She hiked her eyebrows and gave him a knowing look. "I'm a Knife, too, you know. They thought I was the True Son once."

Taemon tried to smile politely. This woman was completely klonkers. And what in the Great Green Earth was that eyebrow thing about? The awkward moment lingered as Taemon turned to Hannova, who gave him a don't-ask-me look.

"Save the scarf for me, Challis? I'll be back for it," Hannova said.

"Yes, you were." Challis nodded and smiled, nodded and smiled.

They moved on.

"Hoy, Taemon!" the baker called from his stand. "When are you coming back to work for me? The herb loaves haven't come out right since you left."

Taemon smiled. "I'm working at the farm now."

Hannova studied Taemon as if she were reading something into his response.

"You let me know when you decide." The baker turned back to his customers.

Hannova led Taemon to the tinker's shop. Taemon had been here a time or two delivering broken farm tools to be mended.

On the walls and from the ceiling hung every imaginable tool, and some that Taemon could never have imagined. Hanging amid the tools were weird pieces of machinery and mysterious gadgets. It reminded him of Da's workshop, only bigger and more chaotic.

Drigg, the tinker, bent over his work, attaching small metal pieces to each other with a heating device of some kind. He didn't look up when Taemon came in with Hannova. They waited for Drigg to notice them.

One of the tools near Taemon looked like it was about to fall off its hook. He reached forward to nudge it back in place.

"Don't touch that!" Drigg yelled, never looking up from his work.

Taemon pulled his hand back. "Sorry," he said. "I thought it was going to fall."

"Ever occur to you it might be hanging that way for a reason?" Drigg asked.

"Sorry," he repeated, flushing.

Drigg switched off his flame tool, examined the swaying

tool, then pushed it securely into place. "I said 'might.'"
He glared at Taemon, switched the flame on, and turned
back to his work.

They waited.

Taemon studied the half-built—or perhaps half-
disassembled—projects lying around. Scattered on the
workbench were bolts and rings, small metal rods about
the length of his pinky finger, a few springs, and the
leavings of a sandwich. A slate hanging above the bench
caught his eye, and he tried to make out the chalked
sketches. It was an engine of some kind, and Taemon
found himself instantly picturing the finished product.

Abruptly Drigg turned off his flame and hung a grimy
rag over the slate. "Something I can do for you?" he
grumbled.

Hannova made the introductions.

"Ah, yes. I remember you," Drigg said. "You're the one
who redesigned Bynon's plow. Like working with tools, do
you?"

"I'm not sure. I never really have before." His eyes wandered back to the slate. "What's the engine for?" he asked.

Drigg hesitated. "Engine?"

Taemon pointed. "If you're going to use cylinders,

seems like you could find a better angle. It's for a byrider, right?"

"A byrider?" Hannova put her fists on her hips. "Have you been scavenging again? We've had this talk before, Drigg. No one's allowed past the drop-off station. Not even you."

"It was only a bit past. This little beauty was lying on the side of the road, begging for me to rescue it." Stepping to the corner of the workshop, Drigg pulled off a tarp to reveal a rusted byrider, the old kind with two wheels, not the unisphere that was popular now.

"It's in rough shape," Taemon said.

"That's where I come in. Building a corn-fueled engine for it." He studied Taemon. "I could use your help, but only if it's what you want. Spending my days with a surly teenager isn't on my list of favorites."

Surly teenager? Is that how Drigg saw him? And how was that any worse than a cranky tinker? Taemon wondered if he would ever manage to fit in anywhere.

"Nothing's decided yet," Hannova said, leading Taemon out the door. "We'll let you know."

Once outside, she took the path that followed the river. They walked for a few minutes in silence. Taemon's head was filled with the sketches he'd seen on the tinker's slate. Already he'd thought of three different changes he'd make to those plans.

"Drigg had a point back there," Hannova said.

"About me being surly?"

"You're not surly," she said. "I'm talking about knowing what you want. Have you figured that out yet, Taemon?"

He hadn't figured that out yet. Not really. That would require settling on one particular future for himself, which he was not ready to do. He looked down at his feet.

Hannova nodded. "I know it all seems pretty overwhelming. But you're a hard worker and you don't cause trouble. I think you'll be happy and successful whatever path you choose."

Taemon almost laughed. Didn't cause trouble? In his mind, he tallied all the troubles he'd caused. When he was four and first learning psi, he set his mind to wandering and accidentally dismantled Da's antique clock. He'd almost murdered his brother. He'd failed his parents by not hiding his disability. He'd let down his only friend. He'd hurt and cheated and disappointed and lied to everyone, including himself.

What he really wanted was to do something right for a

change. And if there was anything he had a remote chance of doing right, it was building an engine.

"I'd like to work with Drigg," Taemon said decisively.

"Excellent. You can have tomorrow off for your birthday and start with Drigg the day after."

They had arrived at Taemon's new home. He stood in front of the door and reminded himself to use the doorknob. Would he ever get used to life without psi?

The next morning, breakfast was unusually quiet. Typically there was a lot of chatter and flubbing around. Enrick and Marka, the married couple that had taken him in, bustled around the kitchen, making sure Taemon and all five of their little ones got fed and everyone had what they needed for school.

In the city, orphans were sent to group homes run by the church. That's what he'd expected in the colony as well, but instead, he'd been taken in by Marka, who was the farmer's daughter. She and her family had been kind to him.

Marka and Enrick's house was a busy place with five young children, two rabbits, a dog, and a fluctuating number of cats. Somebody's milk always spilled. Somebody's eggs usually burned. Yesterday the dog had gotten to the butter dish and licked it clean.

Not today. Today all the little ones sat still. No one teased. No one asked for more cheese. Everyone was eating their breakfast—all too calmly.

Taemon shoveled eggs into his mouth with the pokey thing called a fork. With the last bite in his mouth, he looked up from his plate at the others seated around the table. He saw a twinkle in Marka's eye, a smile playing around Enrick's mouth. The youngest boy started to laugh, but his sister clapped her hand over his mouth. What under Skies was going on?

From behind, someone slapped a blindfold over his eyes. Someone else held him to his chair, and still another someone wrapped him with what felt like strips of cloth.

A storm of laughter blew into the room.

"What? Who?" Taemon struggled, but it was mostly pretend. He could tell this was some kind of prank.

"It's your birthday!"

Taemon recognized the voice of Jad, a kid he'd met while working at the farm. He must be the one tying him to the chair. Kind of a strange birthday custom. Still, it was nice of him to celebrate Taemon's birthday. Jad was a couple of years older and crazy about a girl who worked at the clothier's shop. Taemon didn't have a group of friends in the colony yet. But maybe that could change.

"And not just any birthday." A girl's voice. That had to be the clothier shopgirl, Vangie.

"Thirteen is an unlucky number." A different girl's voice. Now who could that be?

"So I'm being arrested for turning thirteen?" Taemon said.

The little kids giggled. "Arrest Taemon! Arrest Taemon!" they chanted.

"Thanks a lot," Taemon said. "Is this what you do for people on their birthdays? Take them into custody?"

"Just for special cases, like yours," Jad said. "You've had to do more work in your four weeks at the colony than most of us have to do in the first four years after we turn thirteen. So we are officially kidnapping you for the day. Everything's arranged. No work today, no chores."

"You might have told me *before* I made my bed," Taemon grumbled.

One of the little ones giggled.

"We're going on an outing," Vangie said. "A picnic."

The kids' chanting quickened and increased in pitch. "Picnic! Picnic!"

"Sorry, only big kids get to go," Enrick said. "The rest of you have school."

"Aaw."

"I'm a big kid."

"Me too. I big!"

"Somebody get that dog away from the butter!" Marka said.

Taemon's chair was lifted and removed from the din. The chair dipped and lurched as they took him out of the house. If he hadn't been tied down, he would have fallen off by now. He couldn't help thinking that it'd be a whole lot smoother if done with psi.

Outside, Taemon was untied and the blindfold removed. The first thing he saw was a girl's face. She smiled. Her face looked familiar, though he was sure they'd never met. He must have passed her on the street sometime, he decided.

Something else caught Taemon's attention. "Holy Rain! You got the hauler? I thought Bynon said no."

Jad grinned. "Cha, well, Bynon has a soft spot for the

new kid. When I told him it was your birthday, he said we could have it for the whole day."

Taemon was beginning to understand what this birthday outing was all about. For the past week, Jad had been trying to get Bynon, the farm manager, to let him take the hauler so he could take Vangie for a drive. Taemon's birthday was the excuse Jad had needed to get the hauler.

Jad turned to Taemon. "You and Amma hop in the back."

Which meant Jad and Vangie would ride inside the cab. Cha, Jad had a plan, all right. Taemon wondered how Amma felt about this. If she was uneasy, she didn't show it. She climbed into the back of the hauler, brushed the hay aside, and settled herself contentedly on an upturned bucket.

Well, Skies, why not? What else did he have to do on his birthday? Taemon climbed in after her. "Where are we going?"

"It's a surprise," Jad said, and swung himself behind the wheel.

As they bumped and sputtered slowly along the dirt road, Taemon thought there must be a way to cut down the noise on that corn-fueled engine. He'd helped Bynon change the oil on the hauler last week, and he knew the engine could use a lot of work. He pictured it in his mind, mentally diagramming ways to make it run smoothly.

About the time he realized he should probably say something to Amma, she spoke up.

"So today's your birthday," Amma said, half yelling over the noise of the hauler. "One Quake. That's pretty lucky. If you were born the day before, it would have been Thirteen Knife."

Thirteen Knife was the most unlucky day of the calendar. Taemon nodded. "And I was born just after midnight."

Amma laughed. "That must have scared the wits out of your mother."

"That's not hard. She's a Rabbit, so she's jumpy to begin with. What's your birth sign?"

"Water," said Amma. "I always hated it. So boring. Something more glamorous would've been nice, like Flower or Jaguar."

"Water can be powerful." Taemon thought of his battle with the tide in the sea cave.

"Sure, if you enjoy tidal waves or erosion." She shoved him a little, which caught him off guard. Was she mad?

When she chuckled, he realized she was joking with him. Skies, he'd never get used to all these hands-on emotions.

He laughed it off. "Definitely not boring."

The ride was long, and the wind was cold, but it didn't matter. Amma was easy to be with. They talked until the half yelling made them hoarse. Then they played a ridiculous game to see who could spit a piece of hay the farthest. Amma won every time.

"It must be getting close to noon," Taemon said. "Do you know where we're going?"

Amma smiled shyly. "It's this thing Vangie and I like to do. We call it frivolics. We make up these little . . . adventures. Usually it involves some silly little skit, you know, like pretending we're someone else."

"You mean like acting?" Each year a group of youngsters put on a performance at the temple, reenacting Nathan's flight from the Republik and his founding of Deliverance. He wondered if there were similar plays put on in the colony.

"Sort of, but we make it up as we go. No scripts or anything. We work out a general idea ahead of time, but that's all."

"So what's the general idea this time?" Taemon asked.

"This one is Vangie's idea, and she wants it to be a surprise." Amma bit her lip. "I promised not to tell."

Taemon faked outrage. "All right, that's it." He picked up another piece of hay. "All or nothing. If I win this one, you have to tell me. And if you win . . ."

"What?" Amma asked with a smile. "What do I win?"

Taemon looked at the scenery. He wasn't thinking about the hay-spitting game anymore. A deep anxiety worked its way from his stomach to his scalp.

Earth and Sky! Was that the city wall he saw in the distance? They must be way past the drop-off station. He should have been paying attention. He never should've trusted Jad.

Taemon turned and banged on the roof of the driving compartment. "Stop!"

12 QUAKE

Knife retreats as Quake arrives,

Shaking mountains, homes, and lives.

Quake will rattle every pillar.

Quake will humble every builder.

But one who's strong and sound survives.

But one who's strong and sound survives.

— CALENDAR SONG

Before the hauler came to a full stop, Taemon vaulted out of the back and ran to the driver's side. He yanked the door open. "The city? Are you klonkers? We're not supposed to go past the drop-off point!"

"Relax, Taemon. It's going to be fine. First we're going to find a place to hide the hauler. Then we'll have our picnic. After that we'll go for a little walk by the North Gate. I promised Vangie."

"A little walk in the city? You *are* klonkers. Someone will see us!"

"We've got it all worked out, don't we?" Jad turned and smiled at Vangie.

She giggled. "Cha. Amma and I do stuff like this all the time."

"First time this close to the city, though," Amma said with a frown.

"I can't believe this," Taemon said, pacing beside the hauler.

"Help me find a place to hide the hauler," Jad said. "We'll tell you the plan while we eat."

Taemon had a hard time enjoying the picnic. Amma was quiet, too. Jad and Vangie acted like this was a holiday.

Taemon couldn't wait any longer. He needed answers. "What's this big plan of yours?"

"We'll walk through the woods and sneak back to the road near the North Gate," Jad said. "It'll look like we've hiked from another gate."

"They won't let us in," Taemon said. "They'll know we're powerless a mile away. Look at what we're wearing. Loom-woven cloth. Buttons. Shoelaces, for Sky's sake. We look like we're from the Dark Ages."

Jad smiled wryly. "Show him what you brought, Vanj."

"This is my favorite part." Vangie held up a big cloth

bag. "Psi clothes!" One by one she pulled out pants, shirts, shoes, and belts.

"Where'd you get those?" Taemon asked.

"My cousin's an innocent at the temple," Vangie said. "She got them from the lost-and-found and sent them to me. She knows I have a thing for psi clothes."

How insane were these people? Did they really think this would work? "We can't wear psi clothes if we don't have psi to fasten them."

"I've sewn tiny hooks inside the seams," Vangie said. "No one will be able to tell."

"Lighten up a little. It's your birthday." Jad punched Taemon in the shoulder—contact humor again.

Taemon took one of the shirts and examined the hooks. "You don't know anybody in the city. I do. I used to live here, remember? Someone might recognize me."

"Were you famous or something?" Vangie asked. "Did you play psiball? Someday I'm going to find a way to see a psiball match," she added with a dreamy look.

"No, I'm not famous, but still." Taemon thought about his disaster at the psiball tournament a month ago. It had caused quite a stir. Some people might very well recognize him.

"Psiball seems weird," Jad said. "People standing inside a huge glass egg, watching a ball whiz around? Give me a good old basketball game any day."

Vangie pulled out a wide-brimmed hat and handed it to Taemon. "You can wear this. My cousin said it's the latest fashion."

The latest fashion a year ago, maybe. "This is stupid to the power of stupid," Taemon said.

"Why? Who's going to get hurt?" Vangie asked. She held up a shirt for Amma.

Jad tried on one of the belts for size. "No one will know just by looking at us that we're powerless. We won't eat anything; we won't touch anything. We're not even going through the gate. We're just going to blend in with the crowd outside the gate and watch the ceremony."

"Sure," said Taemon. "Blend in. Jad, that belt you're wearing is for a girl. Wait . . . what ceremony?"

Vangie gave him an exasperated look. "Today's the day they announce the True Son."

Skies! How could he have forgotten? In all the trauma of being sent away, he hadn't remembered that the True Son was supposed to be announced on his birthday. Had the high priest chosen Yens? Would Mam and Da be there? He wasn't ready to talk to them, but if he could get a glimpse, just to see if they were okay . . .

"Cha. So exciting. Then they're going to escort him—"

"Or her," Amma said. "It could be a girl."

Vangie rolled her eyes. "Him *or her* through the North Gate, just like the prophecy says, and into the temple."

Taemon's conscience was screaming at him. They were acting way outside their authority. This plan involved breaking at least seventeen rules. So many things could go wrong. On the other hand, he might not have another chance like this. Mam and Da could be just beyond these walls. Could he really turn his back on them?

"Fine. Let's go."

When everyone was dressed as properly as they could manage, the four of them started on foot toward the city. They left the road before anyone could see them, tramped through the trees until they got closer to the crowd, then slipped into the edge of the throng, staying well outside the gate.

Jad was right about the ceremony. A platform had been built a few yards outside of the North Gate, and a crowd had gathered around it. Taemon could see only a little way through the gate, but from the sounds of the crowd, he figured there were quite a few people lining the street inside the city. The True Son would probably lead some kind of processional toward the temple in the center of the city. A few people had ventured outside the gate to get a better view of the platform. Taemon and his friends joined the edge of the crowd without anyone noticing.

Music cut through the noise of the crowd. Crystal shards hung in the air, suspended by psi, striking one another and ringing with a sound as clear as winter dawn. The harmonies were so intricate, no fingers could ever combine that many notes simultaneously.

Taemon looked for his parents. He couldn't see them yet.

He smelled luscious aromas from the vendors' carts. It'd been forever since he'd had a lamb roll. Too bad eating was out of the question.

The psi clothes didn't fit right, and Taemon had to resist the urge to tug at his collar. He looked again for Mam and Da. They must be here somewhere.

The noisy crowd began to settle as an ornately decorated carriage floated in midair toward the gathering. Two lines of temple guards walked behind it as it traveled along the outside of the city wall, no doubt using their psi to lift and propel the carriage. When it passed by, Taemon craned his neck and tried to peer inside, but the thick curtains covered the window. Was it Yens?

Vangie squeezed Jad's arm. "This is so exciting. The True Son must be inside."

As the carriage stopped near the platform, a man stepped up on the stage. Taemon had no trouble recognizing that salt-and-pepper beard entangled with shiny charms, that garish robe—definitely Elder Naseph.

The old high priest turned to face the crowd, his back to Taemon, and began to speak, amplifying his voice with psi. "At last, the True Son is among us!"

The crowd cheered. Taemon had to stop his friends from clapping with their hands. He glanced around to see if anyone noticed, but luckily everyone was fixated on the carriage.

Again he scanned the gathering for his parents. They weren't here. Surely if Yens were the True Son, his parents would be close to the platform. Did that mean Yens hadn't been chosen? Or that Mam and Da objected to the ceremony?

Elder Naseph encouraged the crowd by waving his hands. "The True Son is the greatest among us, yet he desires only to serve. He will bring us into a higher level, an elevated existence. So that you may know the one who is to serve you, I will tell you the remarkable things he has done.

"One day as he played by the ocean with his younger brother, his brother was careless and fell into the sea."

Earth, Sun, and Sky.

It was Yens.

"The True Son ran to get help. But when he came back, he saw that the boy had been sucked into a dangerous sea cave. Everyone thought the boy's life was lost. But the True Son did not give up. He reached into the sea itself, pulled air out of the water, and sent it into the boy's mouth so he could breathe."

How did Elder Naseph know the part about breathing underwater? Taemon had never told anyone, not even Yens.

"When the rescuers carried the boy out of the sea cave, he was barely alive. The True Son nearly lost his life that day as well, so great was the exertion."

An outright lie. And it rolled off Elder Naseph's tongue smooth as honey.

The crowd gasped and oohed. They were sopping it up.

Elder Naseph continued. "This is the selfless sacrifice that characterizes the True Son. His psi is more powerful than any of us has seen, and yet he uses it only for the good of others.

"To you, the true people of the Heart of the Earth, to you I present the leader of the new Great Cycle of power—the True Son!"

The carriage door swung open, and out stepped Yens. The crowd roared its approval. He looked taller, his shoulders a bit broader, his hair longer. And his smile was as smug as Taemon had ever seen it.

"He's so striking!" Vangie gushed. She bounced on her heels like a three-year-old.

He thought about telling his friends that the True Son was his brother. But what if word got back to the whole colony? People might treat him differently, making it harder for him to fit in. And they might want to know all about the True Son, which was the last subject Taemon wanted to talk about. He decided to keep quiet for now.

The crowd hushed as Yens spoke. "True people, this great day falls on Quake—the day of revision. Seeing old things with new eyes. I urge you to see your psi with different eyes. See it as a way to improve our community.

Dedicate your psi to the united vision of the elders, for whatever they ask of you will be for the benefit of all."

It was Yens's voice, but the words sounded stiff, as though the text was memorized or rehearsed. While Taemon listened to the rest of Yens's rousing speech, he watched the high priest and saw him nodding with a lofty air. The priests were up to something; he felt sure of it. But what? And how did Yens fit into their plan? Whatever it was, Taemon was sure it would bring more money into the temple.

Yens's speech concluded, and the crowd cheered again.

"That you may know the extent of his power," Elder Naseph said, "the True Son has a very special display, which shall be the sign that begins the Cycle of Power."

Yens raised his hands and looked up at the sky. His fondness for the dramatic hadn't changed.

The crowd murmured, unsure what was coming.

The ground shook. First a tremble, then the land visibly rolled and buckled. Parts of the wall crumbled. People gasped, laughed, and shouted with delight. Cement chunks from the wall fell toward the crowd, but the flying debris was easily fended off with psi.

An earthquake? How was Yens doing that? A rock about

the size of a watermelon tumbled from the wall, heading directly toward Amma. Everyone saw it. Everyone expected she would whisk it away with psi.

Amma watched with horror. She seemed paralyzed with indecision. Taemon knew exactly what was going through her mind: If she moved out of the way, people would know she was powerless. But if she didn't move out of the way, she'd get hurt and people would still know she was powerless.

At the last moment, Taemon shoved Amma out of the rock's path. In the same instant, the rock abruptly changed direction and tumbled harmlessly away. Someone in the crowd must have helped out with a shove of psi.

It took a few seconds for Taemon to realize what he'd done, the way he'd pushed her with his hands like that. His attempt to keep Amma safe had exposed their powerlessness.

A murmur cascaded through the crowd. Yens turned his attention to the disruption. Across the sea of people, he caught Taemon's eye. Recognition showed on his face, followed quickly by anger.

"Run!" yelled Taemon.

13 DOG

> Quake will quit eventually
> As Dog befriends you readily.
> Dogs will travel in a pack.
> If one is crossed, they all attack.
> So choose your allies carefully.
> So choose your allies carefully.

— CALENDAR SONG

On the way home, Jad and Vangie were laughing it up inside the hauler's cab, no doubt exaggerating the excitement of the day. In the back of the hauler, the mood was different.

"You're sure you're okay?" Taemon asked.

"Cha," Amma said.

"Sorry about pushing you," Taemon said. "I guess I just panicked."

Amma shrugged. "It was an earthquake, after all."

They had made it back to the hauler without any problem. No one had chased them. Yens must have thought sending the guards after them would have meant sharing the center of attention. He wouldn't like that.

"Listen, there's something I want to tell you." Taemon took a breath. Was this really a good idea? Probably not, but something made him plunge ahead. "That guy, the True Son? He's my brother."

"Your brother?" Amma said. "Seriously?"

Taemon nodded. "Don't tell anyone in the colony, okay? I don't want people knowing."

"Cha. Right. If Vangie knew, she wouldn't leave you alone for a second. I won't tell a soul. Skies, he's really your brother?"

"I'm not exactly proud of it."

Amma shook her head. "An earthquake. Can you believe that? Like it's a show or something. Let's hope no one gets bored anytime soon. Tornadoes might be next." She blew her hair out of her eyes. "Psi is a nuisance if you ask me."

"Have you ever had it?" Taemon asked.

Amma turned to him with a shocked expression. "Of

course not. I was born in the colony. They tested me for psi when I was little. That's one test I was happy to fail. They would've sent me to the city."

Taemon remembered how his parents had feared for their children being taken away. He'd never thought about powerless families being in the same situation. "Does that really happen?"

"Not often. They say kids don't develop psi unless they see it every day, think about it, grow up with the assumption that psi is possible. Then, after you're old enough to know that psi exists, it's too late. That part of your brain shuts down or something." She paused. "Do you ever wish you had it back?"

"No," Taemon said firmly. He'd nearly destroyed his family when he had it.

"I just meant . . . Do you like living in the colony?" Amma asked. "When I was in school, the city kids sometimes got teased."

"I didn't have to go to school in the colony," Taemon said.

Amma nodded. "Were they nice to you? The people at the farm, and Marka's family?"

"Cha, nice." Taemon thought he'd answered Amma's question, but she looked at him like she expected more. Like what he had to say actually mattered.

"When I first came here, I thought I would live out the rest of my life in some kind of drudgery. Like a labor camp or something. But people were kind. Marka, Enrick. Their kids acted like I was their favorite cousin come to visit. It was almost *too* nice. I was sent here to be punished, but it doesn't feel like punishment. It feels like . . . like freedom."

Skies, he sounded like an idiot, even to himself!

"Some people have psi. Some don't." Amma shrugged. "It's not like you make a choice."

"I know," Taemon said. "It's just that . . . I didn't expect to like it here, that's all. Tomorrow I'm starting my apprenticeship at the tinker's shop, and I get to fix up a byrider. I'm actually looking forward to it."

Amma was quiet for a while. Then she squinted up at the sky. "If you had the choice, would you choose to go back home?"

Taemon frowned. "It doesn't matter, does it? I'm here to stay, so that's that." Taemon looked away, toward the trees slipping by, shrinking into the distance. But despite his response, the question plagued him. If he woke up tomorrow with psi, would he choose to return to the city? He thought about the greedy priests who didn't help the poor people. Mam and Da afraid of what the neighbors would see, what the healer might report, what the teachers would think. In the colony, things were different. Nothing was locked up. People worked together. Parents held children in their arms. They hugged each other, for Sky's sake.

Amma spoke up, interrupting his confused thoughts.

"I think it does matter," she said. "I think what you want is who you are."

Her words sounded so much like Da. "'The Heart of the Earth judges everyone by the desire of his or her heart.' That's what my da used to say."

"Exactly," Amma said. "What is the desire of your heart? It doesn't matter if you have psi or if you don't. You still have to know what you want; you have to picture it in your head before you can make it happen."

A strange idea struck Taemon. Maybe he had done exactly that. Maybe he had *chosen* to be powerless, rather than live with psi and the burden of deciding who should live and who should die. Here in the colony, with no psi, his life felt more peaceful and settled than it ever had before.

"I *have* chosen the colony," Taemon said.

After that, there was just enough time for one more round of the hay-spitting game, which Taemon lost. Again.

The next morning, Taemon packed his belongings, which amounted to a few clothes plus one of those strange teeth-brushes, and moved into the apprentice's room next to Drigg's workshop. The first week was a bit of a disappointment because they couldn't work on the byrider. Some of the parts had to be tweaked a little more, and Drigg had sent them back to the blacksmith.

Instead, Drigg had been showing Taemon how to use all the different tools he had. Screwdriver. Drill press. Wrench. Even the names sounded violent. Today's tool-of-the-day was pliers.

"Now, I want you to take this"—Drigg handed Taemon a spool of wire—"and use them pliers to make something useful."

Taemon stared at the odd tool the tinker offered him.

"At lunchtime we'll see what you came up with." With

a nod, Drigg tucked his cap over his bald spot and crossed the workshop to start on his own work.

Taemon sighed. He hoped his decision to work for Drigg wasn't a mistake. But going back to Marka's wasn't an option. They were expecting another powerless kid from the city today, a five-year-old girl, and they needed his old room. A new place, a new family, a new school. Taemon remembered how frightened he'd been when he came, and he'd been much older than five. He couldn't imagine being so young and separated from your family and everything you knew.

An idea began brewing in his head. He wanted to make something for Marka and Enrick. Something that would be useful, as Drigg said, but also something that would make the kids smile. Taemon stared at the wire for a second, and when an image came into his mind, he set to work.

Just before noon, Taemon had finished his wire creation. He'd made a row of hooks, the kind you might hang jackets on. He'd twisted and curled the wire to look like a row of whimsical dogs. The hooks were sometimes a tail, sometimes a floppy ear, sometimes a curled tongue.

"Them kids are going to love this," Drigg said.

"Why don't you take it on over? Then take your lunch break."

Taemon nodded. If he remembered right, Amma's house was on the way. He wondered if she was home, and if she'd like to have lunch together. Tucking the hooks inside his jacket, he fumbled with the buttons, then shoved his hands into his pockets as he'd seen the other kids do. The sun was bright for a late winter day, but the air still had a chilly bite.

Marka's house was on the other side of the colony, so Taemon had to walk through the center square. Last time he'd been here was on barter day with Hannova. Today the square looked quiet and deserted. Even though a few shops, like the bakery and the blacksmith, stayed open all week, today was too cold for most people to be out. Taemon saw only one other person, and that was Challis, bundled in one of her colorful scarves. He crossed to the other side of the street and hoped she wouldn't see him.

"Thayer! Oh, Thayer!"

Too late. Challis turned and headed straight for him. He waved but kept walking.

"Come inside and have a hot cup of tea with Auntie Challis."

"Thanks, but another time, maybe. I'm delivering something." Taemon smiled and picked up his pace.

"Ah, yes. The hooks. The Water girl loved them."

Taemon stopped. "The Water girl? You mean Amma?"

"Amma. Yes. That'll be her name."

Taemon blinked in the sun. "How did you know about the hooks?"

"Delightful design." Challis chuckled. "Dogs. So appropriate. You're making friends, aren't you, dear? Skies know you needed them. Knife and Water. Yes, that will make a strong bond. The Water isn't afraid of a Knife, you know. Water and Stone sharpen the Knife."

Even though he knew it was pointless, he couldn't help but try to make sense of what Challis was saying. Knife and Water were birth signs, but why did she think Taemon was a Knife? "That's nice, but I'm a Quake. Always have been."

Challis looked startled for a moment, and Taemon wished he hadn't bothered to argue. He really should have kept walking.

"Oh, dear. They wouldn't have told you, would they? They were afraid for you, dear. The midwife was a friend of your mother's, and . . . well . . . the birth certificate will not be quite correct. You're a Knife, Thayer. A Knife if I ever saw one."

How would she know that? She couldn't know. It wasn't true. Challis was just a mixed-up klonky scarf lady. Arguing with her was useless. It was time to go.

"Okay. Bye, Challis." He smiled a smile that he didn't feel and walked away.

"Good-bye," she called after him. "And remember to go around the back of the Water girl's house. That's the door you've been looking for."

He waved at her without looking back. He was not a Knife. Ridiculous! Yens was a Knife. If Taemon had been born a Knife, both of Mam and Da's two children would have had the most unlucky of all twenty birth signs. And he would have been Thirteen Knife. Unthinkable! Mam would have had a nervous breakdown. And Da would have done something drastic. He would have . . .

Would have done something clearly illegal like altering the birth certificate?

Surely not.

Still, how had Challis known about the hooks?

Amma's large stucco house was built up against the

side of a craggy hill. In fact, the back part of the house seemed to melt into the hill. A covered porch had been built across the front and wrapped around the side of the house. The porch was filled with shelves and shelves, all crammed with pottery. That's what her parents did—they made pottery from clay. Vases, mugs, plates, bowls, pitchers, even decorative artwork. They used their hands to make it, he'd been told. He couldn't help shuddering a bit every time he thought about touching cold, wet clay.

There was a dog on the porch, too. Snoring in a patch of sunlight in front of the door. Taemon hesitated. He wasn't used to dogs and wondered how a person could tell if a dog was friendly or not. Hadn't Challis said something about a door around the back? It couldn't hurt to take a quick look, could it?

He did find a door on the side, near the back. At this point, it was hard to tell where the house ended and the rocky hill began. The door almost looked like it went into the rock itself. But there was something else about this door. Something that wasn't quite right. He peered at it more closely. Other than being old, it looked the same as all the other doors at the colony. A fat, clunky doorknob on one side, three hinges visible on the other side. Something was out of place even though he couldn't name it.

"Taemon? What are you doing?"

Amma's voice pulled him away from his thoughts. He smiled and waved, trying not to look as guilty as he felt. "Just . . . looking for the door."

"Well, the front door's over here. In the front."

He nodded. "Cha, sorry. Remember me? Stupid city kid? I get confused."

"What, the front doors on city houses are around the back?" Amma cocked her head and gave him a sideways glance.

"Well, no, but . . . anyway, I came over to show you this." Taemon showed her the hooks. "I'm on my way to Marka and Enrick's house to give it to them."

Amma's face lit up. "They're adorable!" She gushed over the hooks a bit longer, then her mood became serious. "I have to tell you something."

"What's wrong?" Taemon asked.

She hesitated. "Vangie heard some news . . . from the city. People are . . . are disappearing."

Taemon gripped the hooks tightly. "Disappearing? Who?"

"I'm not sure. Vangie's cousin didn't say." She shrugged. "What do you think it means?"

"I have no idea," Taemon said.

On Taemon's way back from Marka and Enrick's, his head was teeming with uncomfortable thoughts. First Challis had told him he was a Knife, not a Quake, and that his parents had lied about that. He couldn't bring himself to believe it and yet why would she make up something like that? On the other hand, how could she possibly know?

And what Amma had said about people disappearing. That was definitely not good. What was happening in the city? What was the high priest up to? And what was Yens doing? He thought of how Mam and Da hadn't been at Yens's ceremony. Was it an act of protest, or had they been unable to attend?

When he returned to Drigg's workshop, the parts for the byrider were back from the blacksmith. He helped Drigg lay them out, though his mind was still unsettled.

"Have you heard much about what's happening in the

city?" Taemon didn't intend to ask the question, but his thoughts spilled out in words.

Drigg glanced up with a puzzled look. "Just rumors. Mostly about the True Son. He's sixty years old even though he looks sixteen. He can kill people by just looking at them. He has connections in the Republik. Who knows what to believe?"

"Does it worry you?" asked Taemon.

"Nah," Drigg said. "None of that has anything to do with the colony. They've left us alone these two hundred years. Can't think why it would change."

Taemon arranged the gears in order of size, lining them up on the sheet Drigg had laid down. "What about the Republik? Has anyone from the colony been there?" Taemon, like everyone in the city, knew nothing of what lay beyond the mountains. He wondered if the same was true of people in the colony. Not only was crossing the mountains treacherous, but the people of Deliverance were strictly forbidden from traveling to the Republik or having contact with Republikites.

"Well, now, there's a story in that. Years ago, a few brave souls—powerless people, mind you—ventured into the Republik. But the people there never have trusted psi folk, and even when powerless people try to explain that they don't have psi, those Republikites, see, they don't believe it. They figure that powerless is pretty easy to fake and impossible to prove. So they don't allow nobody from this side of the mountains into their lands. Those poor wretches who tried it lost their lives. Save the one they sent back as a message. Nasty tale, that."

"Not one person has crossed the mountains in all those years?" Taemon asked.

"So far's I know. And no one has a mind to cross the ocean. We don't have the resources to build such a ship, and I don't know that the psi folk have the desire. Remember that Nathan was on the receiving end of a whole arsenal of persecution, and nobody wants to relive that."

Geography wasn't something that was taught in the city; it wasn't safe to travel much beyond the city walls, and everything they could ever need was close at hand, so Taemon had never really given much thought to what lay beyond the Republik. But suddenly he found himself curious. "Are there other countries, other republiks, out there?"

Drigg shrugged. "No way to know."

Taemon fiddled with a gear. "So anything could be out there. Doesn't that bother you, not knowing?" Taemon asked.

"Not a lick. If it runs, don't fix it—that's the tinker's creed. Now hand me that chain right there. And be careful!"

Taemon hurried toward Amma's house, dodging the first few drops of a rain shower. He'd promised to help Amma and Vangie with a puppet show for the schoolchildren, and Drigg had agreed to give him the day off. They'd been working on the byrider for a week now and making slow progress.

Outside Amma's place, Taemon saw her and Vangie struggling with a large box. He ran to help, taking the porch steps two at a time.

"Let me," he said, reaching for the box.

"No, I've got this," Amma said. "You go inside and get the other one. It's bigger."

Taemon stepped through the open door. Inside, the room was homey and warm. A fireplace on one side, hand-made braided rugs on the wooden floors, and furniture that looked well worn. But there was stuff everywhere.

Potted plants in homemade ceramics. Children's toys. An abandoned art project, complete with colored pencils scattered around it. Two, no three, musical instruments. And books. Several of them lying here and there, some stacked, some still open. Even one book on the floor, for Skies' sake. Taemon had only laid eyes on a half dozen books in his lifetime. In the city, books were kept locked up in the guilds. Only a person studying for a specific profession could look at them. Even then, tradesmen were only allowed to see the books the guild leaders deemed necessary.

Taemon couldn't help picking up the book on the floor. Right on the cover was a picture of the inside of a human body with each part labeled. Heart! So that's what it looked like. Lungs! Those were the breathing sacs he'd figured out in the sea cave. Esophagus! Did every home in the colony have books like this?

A feeling of guilt filled his chest. Only healers should see these things. He placed the book facedown on the table. Quickly he found the box Amma needed, grabbed it, and rejoined the girls.

"Great. Thanks," Amma said. The three of them headed toward the school to set up the puppet show.

"Want to hear some juicy city gossip?" Vangie said. "You won't believe it. I didn't believe it. But my cousin swears it's true."

"What?" Taemon said.

"The high priest is going to start trading with the Republikites. They're going to send the True Son to meet with them," she said in a rush. "Imagine! Trading with the Republik. I wonder what they wear. What exotic foods they eat. It's so exciting!"

"Hold on," Taemon said. "When is this supposed to happen?"

"Soon," said Vangie. "They're preparing things now."

Could it be true? Was Elder Naseph sending Yens into the Repbulik?

Amma stopped. "Wait! Vangie, did we get the jungle backdrop?"

Vangie frowned. "Didn't you roll it up? I thought it was in the box."

"No, it wouldn't fit." Amma sighed and set down her box. "We'll have to go back and get it."

Taemon glanced back at the house. "I'll go get it. Can I use the back door? That'd be a lot closer."

"There is no back door," Amma said.

"Yes there is. I saw it."

"Oh, that." Amma waved her hand like she was shooing a fly. "It hasn't opened since before I was born."

"Is it locked?" Taemon asked.

"No, just broken." She frowned at him. "This isn't the city. We don't lock things up around here." She looked at Vangie. "Can you carry this the rest of the way? It's probably easiest if I go grab the backdrop."

"Sure," Vangie said, taking sole hold of the box she'd been carrying with Amma. Just then, the rain started picking up. Taemon and Vangie quickened their pace.

By the time they found the stage and started pulling puppets out of the boxes, Amma arrived. "Vangie, can you get this jungle backdrop up right away? Taemon, help me move this table to the center," Amma said. "We're on first."

Taemon picked up his end of the table. Together they shuffled toward the center of the stage, just behind the main curtain. "Maybe I could take a look at that door sometime," Taemon said, watching Vangie hook the backdrop in place. "I bet I could fix it."

"That's okay," Amma said. "We never use it, so it doesn't matter that it's broken."

"Still, it wouldn't hurt to try."

Amma dropped her end of the table with a loud thump. "Would you forget about the door already?" She blew her hair out of her face. "Come on, we've got to finish setting up."

Taemon and Vangie exchanged a look. "Sorry," he muttered. Taemon tried not to think about the door. He had other things to worry about, like why the high priest would send Yens to trade with the Republik.

They arranged the puppets under the table and then checked the backdrop one last time. On the other side of the curtain, the announcer called for quiet. The program was about to begin. More quickly than Taemon expected, the room quieted down.

The curtain parted.

"We're on," whispered Amma.

The puppet show was an animal version of a story told in the scriptures. A jaguar gets caught in a trap, and none of the other animals want to help him. Amma was the narrator while Taemon and Vangie did the animals' voices. He'd had great fun with the animal voices during their practices, but now he couldn't concentrate. Why would

Elder Naseph all of a sudden decide that trading with the outside world was a good idea? What did he expect Yens to bring back? Amma nudged him. "The jaguar," she whispered.

"Brother Turtle, surely you can help me," Taemon said in a gruff voice.

"Did I hear something?" Vangie made the turtle's voice deep and lilting. "Must have been the wind."

Why would the high priest suddenly decide to trade with the Republik? What did he want that he didn't already have?

"Sister Serpent, please help me," Taemon made the jaguar say.

Vangie hissed. "What can I do? I don't even have armsss."

Da wouldn't take kindly to making contact with the Republik. He'd have something to say about that. Had he spoken out? Was that why he and Mam hadn't been at Yens's ceremony?

Another nudge from Amma. "Brother Mouse, please help me," Taemon said for the jaguar.

Suppose his da and mam *had* disappeared. What did

that even mean? Where had they gone? Were they all right? If only there were some way he could know what was happening. "Flame it all!"

Skies! Had he said that out loud? Loud enough for people to hear? It was a mild curse, but definitely not within the range of appropriate. Not for a kids' puppet show. And a religious one at that.

The audience roared with laughter.

Taemon felt his face redden. He was supposed to do the mouse voice, too. What was the mouse supposed to say? He couldn't think what came next.

Amma glared at Taemon.

For all the Great Green Earth, he couldn't remember anything they'd practiced. He'd have to make something up. He turned the mouse puppet to face the audience.

"What do you think I should do, boys and girls?" Taemon asked in his squeaky mouse voice. "Should I help Brother Jaguar?"

The kids clapped and yelled in the affirmative.

"I don't know," Taemon made the mouse say. "He has awfully sharp teeth. You really think I should help him?"

"Yes!" the kids yelled.

"Are you sure? Have you seen the size of his claws?"

"Yes!" Each response increased in volume.

Amma wasn't glaring anymore—she even laughed. Going along with Taemon's improvisation, she made up silly lines for the narrator. By the time they finished, even the teachers were chuckling. The show ended to thunderous applause.

When the curtain closed, Vangie took down the backdrop while Taemon helped Amma move the table to the back of the stage, behind the last row of black curtains. He could still hear the clapping. He looked at her face, shadowed and gray, and she had that familiar look about her again. As if he had known her from a long time ago.

That was impossible. She had never lived in the city. He shook the thought from his head.

They set the table down. Taemon started gathering puppets.

"You were wonderful!" Amma said, beaming. "We do that puppet show every year, but it's never been that much fun. Come on, it's time for our bow."

She reached out and took his hand. He dropped the

puppets. She was holding his hand. With her hand. No one had ever done that to him before. It was the strangest, most fascinating feeling, warm and comforting and tingly all at once. Then she led him toward the front of the stage, where Vangie was. The three of them stood in front of the curtain now while everyone clapped.

Before Taemon even knew what was happening, Vangie took his other hand. Skies, he was standing in front of an audience holding hands with two girls. They bowed. That is, Vangie and Amma bowed as Taemon stood there, paralyzed. The audience was smiling and clapping, the two girls were beaming and bowing, and Taemon had to remind himself to take another breath.

The rain had stopped. On the way back to Amma's house with the boxes, the mood was light and sunny.

"You know what I think?" Vangie said when they got to the porch. They set the boxes down and sat on the steps. "I think we need to plan our next frivolics."

"Yes!" Amma said. "What should we do this time?"

"I picked the last one," Vangie said. "It's your turn."

"Okay, I can come up with something." Amma smiled. "Are you in, Taemon?"

"I'm in," he answered. "Just don't make me memorize any lines. And no more trips to the city."

They chatted on the steps until it was time for Taemon to go home. Vangie was spending the night at Amma's house, so the two girls went inside. When he left, Taemon paused on the side of the house and stared at the door that didn't open. He bet he could borrow the tools from Drigg to fix it. Colony doors were pretty simple things. How broken could it really be?

He studied the door, wondering if it was the doorknob that was broken. There were all sorts of doorknobs in the colony, from smooth round things to simple hooks and latches to more complicated contraptions, but they were all rather simple from a mechanical point of view. In the city, on the other hand, all psi doors had the same latch. If you wanted anybody to be able to open a door, you had to have the standard door latch. Everyone knew what this latch looked like and could envision it well enough to lift the lever and open the door. In school, one of the first things they taught you was how to open doors. The teacher had a model door latch—without the door around it—and the kids had to study until they could open it with psi. Very simple. As long as you had psi.

If it wasn't the doorknob that was busted, though, what else could it be? Were the hinges rusted? The door *was* exposed to the elements.

As he stood there wondering what was wrong with the door, Taemon felt his mind itching to wander into that door and figure it out. He hadn't tried mind wandering in a long time—not since the sea cave. But almost without realizing it, his body relaxed and his mind traveled out toward the door.

And saw inside it.

Saw that the doorknob was a fake.

Saw inside the wood, which concealed a layer of thick steel.

Saw what was really keeping the door closed.

Deep inside the heart of the door was a psi lock—the most complicated psi lock he'd ever seen. If he studied it long enough, he might be able to open it. Automatically, he reached out with psi to move one of the lock's pins.

Be it so!

But nothing happened. He almost laughed at himself. What had he expected? That just because he could still do the mind-wandering thing he'd be able to use psi, too?

Besides, it was better this way, Taemon told himself. Without psi, mind wandering was pretty harmless. Useless, even. But still weird.

Weirder yet—what was an old psi door doing in a powerless colony?

14 OWL

Dog departs, and in Owl wings.

Silently he watches things.

His sharp senses serve him well.

He knows things that he'll never tell.

But seeing is not everything.

But seeing is not everything.

— CALENDAR SONG

One month had passed since Taemon became Drigg's apprentice, and the byrider's engine was still in pieces. They'd fixed the body—that had been easy. Getting the corn-fueled engine to work was a different story. It seemed that every time he and the tinker got one part of the engine to work, a different part didn't work anymore. Taemon had lost track of how many times he had delivered and retrieved parts from the smithy's shop. And today he was headed there again.

The weather had warmed up, and even though the air felt a little nippy, people were happy to be outdoors.

"Thayer! Oh, Thayer!"

Taemon cringed, then turned around to see Challis. She had moved her loom to her front porch and was waving him over. "You'll come have a cup of tea with Auntie Challis. You promised."

Better just get this over with. He headed across the street.

Once Taemon was there, Challis was unusually quiet. She stared at him with a vacant look. This woman was more loopy than knots.

"Um, that's a nice scarf you're weaving," said Taemon.

"Wait until you've seen the ones I'll make next week. You sat here and watched my loom for me while I got us each a mug of tea." She went inside.

Sat? Watched? That was another annoying thing about Challis. She was always using the wrong verb tenses. He wondered what kind of tea she was making.

He studied the cloth on her loom and found it mesmerizing. He followed one thread, a bright green strand, as it looped and zigzagged through the weave. Was is part of a pattern? If so, he couldn't tell what it was yet.

Challis came out with two earthenware mugs. He recognized them as being made by Amma's family. Taemon took the one she handed to him, lifted it up, and sniffed. The mug felt warm, and the tea smelled citrusy sweet.

Taemon hesitated. Some things were still hard for him to get used to. Putting your mouth on someone else's cup? It was hard enough to put his mouth on his own cup even when he knew no one else ever used it. But he knew it was bad manners to pour liquid into his mouth. He examined the cup's rim. Was it clean? Probably not. No one had any psi to clean things the real way.

"Um, very nice," said Taemon. "Thanks." He stared at the cup. He licked his dry lips but couldn't bring himself to drink.

Challis put a hand on Taemon's shoulder. She had a faraway look in her eyes again. "Renda," she said.

The sound of Mam's name shocked him. "You knew my mother?"

Challis smiled. "Your mother, my sister. Did you know your eyebrows look exactly like our father's? His name was Thayer."

She wasn't just off her rocker. She was off her planet. "Mam's sister died when she was four."

"Mm-hmm. Sometimes they say that so as to avoid the upsetting of reputations. You know our family, direct descendants of Nathan and all. Couldn't have imbeciles in the family tree, now could we?"

Taemon thought about that. He wondered whether his parents would have told everyone that he died if his disability hadn't been revealed in such a public way.

"Now then. You and I had a little chat. Right here." Challis patted one of two cushioned rockers and then sat down in the other. The chair's cushion was embroidered with flowers.

Taemon sat down in the flower chair. Not because he wanted to chat, but because he needed to think about this. Was Challis telling the truth? How could he know? She was right about his mother's name and the family descending from Nathan. Mam never talked much about her parents, and so he had no way of knowing if his grandfather's name had been Thayer. But he supposed such information wasn't exactly secret. Did Challis have a contact in the city who was feeding her information?

"I need to explain some things." Challis sipped her tea. "You'll be confused. I get beginnings mixed up with endings sometimes."

"I'm already confused. So start wherever you like."

"I came to the colony as a young child. Raised by a family that adopted me. The priests said I didn't have any psi, but that wasn't exactly true."

"You do? You did?"

Challis tsked. "Watch those verb tenses, son. You'll confuse people that way. Yes, I have psi. But not the way they see it."

Taemon shook his head. "I don't understand."

Challis leaned forward in her chair. "Psionic power can take a number of forms, each one a scientifically inexplicable transfer of energy or information."

Strangely, Challis's voice took on a certain authority. Taemon had no doubt that at this moment, she knew exactly what she was talking about. Goose bumps dotted his arms.

"Psychokinesis. Telepathy. Remote viewing. Clairvoyance. Psychometry. Precognition." She ticked them off on her fingers. "Those are the six known forms of psi. Some scholars theorize that there may be a seventh."

"Forms of psi? I'm not following you."

"Psychokinesis, that's what everyone thinks of as psi. The ability to influence physical objects with your mind. Moving things, shaping things without touching them."

"Right. That's what psi is."

"Wrong. That is the most common way that psionic ability manifests itself. It's what all the psi wielders use in the city. But there are other, rarer, forms of psi. Anyone with any of the other powers is thought to be dangerous. What's the phrase? A loose cannoli?"

"I think you mean a loose cannon."

"Exactly. I didn't have psychokinesis, but I had other forms of psi. Remote viewing, precognition. They didn't know what to do with me. One of the priests even thought I might be the True Son." She chuckled. "I went through all kinds of tests to see what I could do. When they found out I couldn't do what they wanted, they sent me here. I was four years old. I was lucky."

"Lucky?"

"They could just as easily have killed me. Someone whose powers are different is, well, an unknown factor. Very dangerous. A loose candle."

Skies, all this was actually making sense. She had to be telling the truth. There was no possible way she could have made all this up. But Taemon was having a hard time sorting it all out. "Precognition? That would be . . . knowing something before it happened?"

Challis nodded. "You'd be surprised at how confusing that is. I learn things that I haven't remembered yet. I'll remember things I haven't forgotten yet. Then I forget things that I haven't learned yet."

That explained why Challis couldn't keep her verb tenses straight.

She smiled at him, and it reminded him of Mam. Why hadn't he ever noticed that before? "You were a loose cannibal, too," she said. "Before you quit your psi, anyway."

"Quit? Is that what I did?"

She nodded. "You quit one kind of psi and kept the other."

"I only had the regular kind. What'd you call it?" Taemon frowned. "Psychokinesis."

Challis shook her finger in Taemon's direction. "Which boy will figure out how to drive the unisphere? Which boy found oxygen atoms in the water inside the sea cave? Who sees the psi door at Amma's house? Psychokinesis doesn't do that; clairvoyance does. Clairvoyance, the ability to perceive things without using the five senses. *Very* rare. Unheard of, really."

Skies above! That mind-wandering thing had a name. No wonder Da wanted to make sure Taemon never used mind wandering. It might have gotten him killed if anyone knew what he had been able to do. "Wait, how do you know about that? I never told anyone!"

Challis smiled. "Remote viewing? It means seeing things that happen far away. Don't you think I'd keep an eye on my nephews?"

The full impact of what Challis was saying hit him like a wall of flame. If Challis had been watching him over the years, that meant the thing about him being a Knife was probably true. Why hadn't his parents ever told him? A person's whole identity was wrapped up in his birth sign. Who was Taemon if he wasn't One Quake? If he was Thirteen Knife, the unluckiest sign of all?

If Challis knew about his birth sign and the unisphere and the sea cave, then she probably knew about the time he'd almost killed Yens. Another thought struck him: Had it been *her* voice he'd heard in his head those times? It had sounded nothing like her speaking voice, but then maybe speaking voices were different than mental voices. She had told him he could kill Yens. Yens, her own nephew! Worse yet, he'd almost done it! Skies, he couldn't decide which of them was the bigger loon!

"When virtue is missing, power must be separated from knowledge," Challis said.

Taemon had no idea how to respond to that. Luckily, Challis kept talking.

"That's one answer," she said. "But you have your own questions. So ask."

He didn't want to talk about what he'd done to Yens. Or about his birth sign or the mind wandering that made him so dangerous. Instead, he asked the question that until recently had been dominating his thoughts. "Why is there a psi door at Amma's house?"

"Yes, that is the perfect question." She sat back in her chair and closed her eyes. "And here she is right now to answer you."

A few silent seconds passed as Taemon looked around. "I don't see anyone."

Opening her eyes, Challis sat up and looked this way and that. "She's late. The ocean is always on time. Hasn't she heard of the tides?"

"Do you mean Amma?" Taemon asked. "Did you ask her to come?"

"I didn't have to ask her. I saw her come. She should be here by now. Timing is everything." Challis squirmed in her seat.

"It's okay," said Taemon. "I'm sure she's on her way."

No sooner had the words left his mouth than he spotted Amma walking toward them.

"There you are," she said to Taemon. "I've been looking for you."

Taemon glanced at Challis, who looked relieved. "Challis and I have been having a very interesting chat," he began.

"Do you finally believe that she's your aunt?" Amma asked before Taemon could fill her in.

Taemon's jaw dropped. "How did you—? Did she—?" He glanced between Amma and Challis.

Amma smiled at him. "I'll explain everything on the way to my place. You're to have dinner with us tonight. Mam and Da are expecting you."

He had about a million questions, but only one made it past his mouth: "Will there be cucumbers?"

Amma laughed. "No cucumbers. I promise."

•   •   •

It was hard not to be nervous about eating dinner with the Parvel family. Taemon had met Amma's parents once or twice — the colony wasn't that big — but this was the first time he'd have a real conversation with them. And family meals were never his strong suit.

He stared down at the big chunks of vegetables and beef in his bowl. It smelled delicious. Hearty and simple. And not one cucumber in sight. Taemon picked up his spoon, then put it down again. Was he supposed to use the fork or the spoon for stew? The eating tools were familiar to him by now, but psiless table manners were still a bit of a mystery. He took a chance and grabbed the spoon again and scooped a hunk of potato into his mouth. It was on the big side, and some of the broth trickled down his chin. Where was that napkin?

Amma stifled a giggle. "Don't worry, Taemon. As long as everyone's full after the meal, Mam's happy."

Taemon found himself relaxing as the meal went on. So far, no one had mentioned the old door. Maybe Challis was wrong about why Amma had been looking for him. Maybe this was just to be a friendly evening spent with her and her family.

"That was incredible, Mrs. Parvel. Thank you," Taemon

said when he had finished. He helped clear the table and offered to help wash the dishes, but Mrs. Parvel wouldn't hear of it.

"Let's sit down and chat about the door," said Amma's da, leading Taemon into the sitting room.

Amma went ahead of them to rearrange the books, papers, and art supplies so they could sit comfortably.

"I have to admit," Mr. Parvel said, "I wasn't pleased when Challis came to me and told me I needed to show you what is behind our psi door. But Challis was pretty insistent, and Amma says you're trustworthy. It's just that, well, you having lived so long in the city, that makes me nervous."

So it *was* a psi door, and Amma's family knew it. Taemon was both curious and confused. What could the colony possibly need to keep behind such a powerful door? And how did Mr. Parvel expect to show Taemon what was behind a psi door when no one had the psi to open it? Had Challis misled them, made them think he still had the useful type of psi?

Amma huffed. "Da, you can't hold that against him."

"I know how you feel about it, Amma, but we have to be so careful. If the wrong people found out about the door, well, it would be devastating." Mr. Parvel looked

Taemon in the eye. "I have to know for certain, son. Will you stand behind the colony no matter what? Can I trust you absolutely?"

Taemon held Mr. Parvel's gaze. "If you're asking me if I would betray the colony, the answer is no. Never."

A moment passed in which Mr. Parvel looked straight at Taemon. Now was not the time to look away or flinch. He held steady without so much as a blink.

"All right, then. If Challis says you need to see this, then let's get to it." Mr. Parvel walked out of the room. Taemon looked at Amma, and she gestured for him to follow her da. Amma walked behind him.

He followed Amma's da out the front door and around to the back of the house. Mr. Parvel glanced about to see if anyone was nearby, and Taemon found himself doing the same. When he looked back at the door, it was open.

"Wait, how did you . . . ?" Taemon rubbed his temples. So much to take in. "You have psi?"

Amma nodded. "My whole family does. But we only have authority to use it to protect the library. My brothers and I, we all learned psi when we were little, and on our thirteenth birthday, we take the vow and dedicate our psi to protecting the library."

"The what?" Taemon asked.

Mr. Parvel smiled and gestured forward with a nod. "Now I'll show you where it leads."

As they passed through the door, Taemon could see from the inside just how strong the door was. Thick metal frames melded into incredibly solid rock. Not even psi could pull this door off its hinges. No one was getting through this door without knowing the lock's sequence. He followed Mr. Parvel through a hallway that narrowed, and the light grew dimmer. When they stepped into a large room, Amma switched on a light.

Books. Shelves and shelves. Stacks and stacks. Thick, thin, tall, short—Taemon didn't think this many books still existed. Was this a school of some kind? He walked toward a cart that held even more books and examined them.

Owls: A Guide to Their Behavior and Biology

Secrets of a Master Violinmaker

The Complete Book of Plant Propagation

Effects of Education on Labor Supply

Taemon stood amazed at the wealth of knowledge in one room.

He picked up *Diseases of the Inner Ear* and thumbed

through it. Diagrams, sketches, explanations, causes of dizziness, it was all there. Absolutely astonishing. He had no idea that the inside of his ear was such a complicated system. Taemon knew that if he studied this book for a few days, he'd be able to use his psi to cure most earaches. If he had psi, that was.

"So many books," Taemon whispered. Even though he had permission to be there, he couldn't help feeling that he was doing something illegal. In the city, he'd never be allowed to see books like these. They would be locked up in the safe at the healers' guild.

He picked up another book. *How Glass Is Made.* He scanned a few pages. With this, he could make windows, windshields, bottles—if he had psi.

Taemon's emotions were an odd combination. The thought of all this knowledge in one place, the things that he could do once he understood how things worked, the wealth this room held—all that was sweet. Then came the bitter realization that without psi, the knowledge was inert. Still interesting, but not something he could act on. It was sad, in a way. So much understanding in a place where no one could do anything with it.

"It's beautiful, isn't it?" Amma whispered.

"All these books," said Taemon. "What are they for?"

"There's a word for a room like this. It's called a library." Amma looked around and smiled.

"Library," Taemon repeated, the word dancing across his tongue. "But why does it have to be secret? Since nobody in the colony has psi, why keep the books hidden away?"

"Do you know what an atom is?" Mr. Parvel asked.

"No," Taemon said. But the word sounded familiar. Hadn't Challis said something about atoms—atoms he'd taken from the water?

"Amma, fetch me—"

"Here it is, Da," Amma said, handing her father a book she'd slipped from a nearby shelf. Mr. Parvel passed the book to Taemon.

"Understanding the Atom," he read from the book's spine.

"Everything in the world is made up of tiny building blocks called atoms," Mr. Parvel explained. "Trust me when I tell you this: if you knew what an atom is and how it works, and if you had psi, you could rip the entire planet to shreds."

Taemon thrust the book back toward Mr. Parvel.

"Okay, but why would anybody want to rip their planet to shreds? That's pretty stupid."

"It is indeed. But humankind has done some pretty stupid things throughout history. Just think of the Great War and all its devastation. Think of how Nathan was treated. Just because someone has knowledge of how something works doesn't mean he or she fully understands it. That person might destroy the world accidentally. Or maybe try to rip only part of the planet to shreds. The part where their enemies live."

Taemon's eyes grew wide. Mr. Parvel's point was beginning to dawn on him.

"This room is only a part of the library," Amma explained. "There are twelve rooms, most of them bigger than this. Deep in caves of this hill. We have thousands of books here, some collected by Nathan himself. Actually he created the library first, even before he started the city and before he created Mount Deliverance. Since then, my family has been collecting and cataloging books, many of which have been smuggled into the colony from the city. Knowledge from every age."

Mr. Parvel nodded slowly. "Imagine for a moment that the psi wielders gained access to this. They would have unlimited knowledge to combine with their unlimited power. What do you think would happen?"

"Chaos," breathed Taemon. "Ruin. Disaster. But there aren't any psi wielders in the colony, except for you and Challis, right? So the library is safe?"

"For the most part, yes," Mr. Parvel said. "Only people who truly need the books are allowed access. And even then, only people we know we can absolutely trust. The temptation to spread rumors about the library or to sell the information to the priests in the city is too great for many to resist."

Amma took the book from Taemon and placed it back on the cart. "That's my family's job: to keep the library safe."

"I thought . . . you made pottery."

Amma laughed. "That's my mom's job. The rest of us protect the library. The stone walls and the psi lock help keep the library safe. No one but my family knows the combination. And we're sworn to guard it with our lives."

Taemon swallowed. Technically, he was a psi wielder. Because of his clairvoyance. He glanced over at Mr. Parvel, who was studying his reaction to all this. They had trusted him with their secret. He should probably trust them with his. "Listen, there's something I —"

Mrs. Parvel came bursting into the room. "Challis is here and wants to talk to you. She says it's urgent."

Mr. Parvel sighed. "What now?"

The three of them filed back through the psi door, which either Amma or Mr. Parvel locked behind them, and found Challis nibbling a slice of sweet tuber tart at the kitchen table.

"Ah, Thayer. I came to collect you. You will have learned enough for one night, yes?"

Came to collect him? Challis seemed to be orchestrating this entire evening.

"I was hoping to talk to Mr. Parvel a little more. I still have a lot of questions."

"Yes, yes, but not tonight. Trust me. Auntie knows best."

The next frivolics were set for six days later, and Taemon welcomed a little diversion. He still hadn't been able to find a way to tell Amma about his psi. How would he explain it? Would she even believe him? If he could talk to her alone today, he would try.

Amma hadn't told him anything except to meet her,

Vangie, and Jad next to the fountain in the square at five o'clock that evening.

At the square, the first thing Taemon noticed was a boat floating in the water that surrounded the fountain. It was a child's boat, only big enough for two people, maybe three if you sat down and let your legs dangle over the sides.

Taemon laughed. What had Amma cooked up this time?

He looked around but didn't see his friends. That was okay. He was a few minutes early.

Taemon sat on the cement bench that surrounded the fountain and pulled out his journal. Maybe if he sketched the workings of the psi lock, he would have proof of his clairvoyance. As he drew the pins and wheels and bolts, the unlocking sequence began to come to him. He was only a squinch away from solving the sequence to that lock.

He drew the psi lock once again.

Even if he figured it out, he wouldn't be able to open it. But he still needed to solve the puzzle, to crack the code. His mind wouldn't let it alone. When he drew it a third time, he saw it. The only sequence that made sense.

Skies! He'd never seen anything like that before. He had no way to test it, but he was certain he'd found the right sequence. He could feel it.

"Hoy, Taemon." Vangie startled him as she sat down. He dropped his journal, and she bent down to pick it up. "What's this?"

Before he could answer, she was thumbing through it. He felt panic rise through his spine. The library's lock was in there!

"Cool," Vangie said, twisting her body so that the journal was out of his reach. "Wow, what's this one? A byrider with one wheel? It uses psi, doesn't it? So flaming cool!" She flipped forward a few pages. "Oh, Skies. Look at that! But what is it?" She stared at his drawings of the psi lock, her brow furrowed.

"It's nothing," Taemon said, snatching the journal back and stuffing it into his jacket pocket. Time to change the subject. "Have you seen Amma yet?"

"Cha. She's headed this way." Vangie pointed across the square.

Amma walked up and handed him an old-fashioned sailor's jacket and cap. Only the Good Earth knew where she'd dug those up. She saluted. "Ahoy, Captain! Let me introduce you to the mighty *Sea Flea*. We're giving free boat rides today."

"Me? Captain?" Taemon asked. "How can I move a boat without psi?"

Amma rolled her eyes. "Ever heard of an oar?"

"Or? Or what?"

Vangie and Amma laughed, but Taemon shrugged. How under Blue Skies was he supposed to know these things?

Amma walked over to the boat, reached in, and pulled out a stick, the bottom half of which had been flattened. "This"—she held the stick high and shook it—"is an oar. You use it like so"—she waved it next to her side—"to move the boat forward."

Taemon grimaced. "Can't someone else be the captain?"

"Don't look at me," Vangie said. "That jacket's navy blue. Thoroughly not my color."

Amma snorted.

"What?" Vangie asked. "I'm a Flower. Appearances are important to me."

"I was really hoping you'd do it. Come on, Taemon. It'll be good for you. Look, the water's only a few inches deep, so you can use the oar like a pole and push off the bottom to move the boat. It's not that hard."

The water *did* seem pretty shallow. And unlike the ocean, there was no current in the fountain. He pushed aside his reluctance and forced a smile. "Okay. I'll do my best."

"Great!" Amma said. "Put on the jacket and cap."

Taemon took off his own jacket, patted the pocket to make sure the journal was still there, then rolled it up and tucked it under the bench. Slipping on the captain's jacket, he nodded as Amma explained in more detail what she wanted him to do. By the time she had finished, the square was filling up with people. It was the time when people milled around the square, talking and relaxing between work and dinner.

When Jad finally showed up, Amma held a big cone-shaped thing up to her mouth. "Ladies and gentlemen! May I have your attention, please? This evening we are pleased to present the newly christened *Sea Flea*, with Captain Taemon at the helm."

Taemon stood in a stoic posture, one foot in the boat and the other on the rim of the fountain's pool. With what he hoped was a manly look, he saluted the crowd.

Amma grinned at him. "Captain Taemon will be taking passengers on a boat tour of the colony. You haven't seen the colony till you've seen it from the water!"

Vangie was the first passenger, and Jad's role was to give a short safety lecture, which included the proper use of something called a life jacket.

Each time Taemon sailed his wobbly course around the fountain, he felt a little more confident. Amma was right. It wasn't so hard. Once he had relaxed a bit, he even added a little narration. "In the distance, you will see the majestic Mount Deliverance in all its glory, and to your right, Manchee's Shoe Shop."

Finally there was only one more child in line. It was the little girl who had come from the city just a couple of weeks ago. Her name was Kivvy. Taemon remembered how happy she'd been when she'd seen the hooks he made. Between that and the fact that they'd both been kicked out of the city, he found he had a bit of a soft spot for little Kivvy. She'd waited a long time in line, and Taemon wanted to give her a nice ride.

"My tuhn?" she asked.

Taemon nodded and helped her into the boat. "Do you want to go fast or slow?"

Kivvy smiled. "Fast. Vewy fast."

"Okay," he said. "Here we go!"

Taemon pushed off, and around the fountain they went.

Kivvy laughed, and that warmed him all the way through. "How are things at Marka's house?" he asked. "Is the dog behaving himself?"

Kivvy nodded. "I used to have a cat. In my psi house."

"What was her name?" Taemon asked.

"Boodle. Mam said she ran away, but I think the bad men took her just like they took Mr. Allet. And Mrs. Murney."

So people really were disappearing. Who was taking them? And why?

They were back where they had started. Taemon tried to think of something that would end Kivvy's ride on a happy note. As Amma helped the little girl out of the boat, Taemon removed his hat and attempted an elaborate, silly bow. But he lost his balance, wheeling his arms in an effort to stay in the boat. He lost the contest with gravity and fell backward into the water.

The water was deep enough to cover his face. Sunlight broke through the surface in splinters of rainbow, then his vision went dark. He was back in the sea cave. He couldn't breathe. He was trapped. No, this wasn't the sea cave. This was someplace different, someplace much, much worse. Someone was about to kill him. No, wait.

It wasn't Taemon that was about to be killed. It was Yens. The Republikites had Yens, and they were going to kill him. **You must decide,** someone was saying. **Think carefully. You must decide.**

Two hands reached through the water, grabbing his jacket and yanking him upward. "Are you okay?"

He sat up, wiped the water out of his eyes, and looked up to see Amma's face.

People were staring at him.

He couldn't remember why he was in the water.

Kivvy giggled. "Funny Taemon. Do it again!"

Everyone laughed, and the tension broke. Taemon remembered now about the frivolics and the boat rides.

"C'mon, Kivvy," Amma said. "We'll let funny boy dry off. I'll give you another boat ride, if you'd like."

Taemon fished the hat out of the water and sloshed out of the fountain's pool. He took deep breaths. What had happened? Some kind of anxiety episode?

After Kivvy's second ride was over, Amma tied up the boat and came over to Taemon.

"You scared me," Amma said. "When you fell in, you didn't move. You just lay there with your eyes open."

Taemon ran a hand through his wet hair. "Cha, sorry

about that. I, um, had a bad experience with water not too long ago."

Amma stifled a laugh. "Sorry. I shouldn't laugh, but you know, my birth sign is Water."

"Never boring." Taemon smiled and looked down at his shoes, which were creating rivulets on the cobblestones. He peeled off the wet captain's jacket and handed it to Amma, then retrieved his own jacket. He wasn't ready to talk to Amma about clairvoyance just yet. Maybe tomorrow.

Taemon woke up early the next day, determined to find a way to talk to Amma. He'd show her the drawings in his journal and explain everything. She had trusted him enough to tell him about her abilities, and he should do the same. Taemon dressed quickly and grabbed his jacket. If he hurried, he could be back before Drigg even got out of bed.

When he reached in his pocket for his journal, he felt nothing. Maybe the other pocket? It wasn't there either. A quick search of his room yielded nothing. Had it fallen out on the way home yesterday? Skies, now he had two things to confess to Amma: one, that he had a strange form of psi called clairvoyance. And two, that he'd drawn her family's psi lock but had lost the drawing somewhere in town!

Taemon started off toward Amma's house. If he was able to convince her that he had clairvoyance, perhaps she would help him look for the journal. Thankfully, anyone who found it wouldn't be able to make head or tail of his sketches and notes. Not without psi.

Standing at the front door, Taemon hesitated. He knew how hard it had been for Amma's da to trust him. How much harder would it be once he heard what Taemon had to tell him?

Taemon raised his hand to knock, which was a rather painful thing psiless people had to do when they wanted to enter someone else's home. But before he could knock, Amma opened the door.

She looked worried. "I was just going to get you," she said.

Behind her came the sound of loud voices. Upset voices.

"Why?" Taemon asked. "What's wrong?"

"It's Vangie. She's run away."

15 FLOWER

Owl is done when Flower blooms,

With charm and grace and sweet perfume.

His beauty draws the eye's attention

With the truth or with pretension.

He may not be what you assume.

He may not be what you assume.

— CALENDAR SONG

Amma led Taemon into the kitchen, where her parents, Vangie's parents, and Hannova sat around the table. They all looked tense and worried.

Vangie's mother wrung her hands. "She's obsessed with psi—psi fashion, psiball, temple gossip. She wanted to be an innocent in the temple with her cousin, but I wouldn't let her. I'm sure she's gone to the city."

"If that's true," Hannova said, "we should be able to find her. I can talk to the priests. We can bring her back."

Amma frowned. "She's talked about running away before. I never thought she was serious. Why would she leave now?"

"Our little Flower," said Vangie's mother. "Skies watch over her."

Hannova put her arm around Vangie's mother. "I'll send a runner. We'll set up a meeting with the priests. Temple innocents are required to get parental permission. And there are fees for room and board. They won't take her in without that. Did she take anything valuable with her?"

"No," Vangie's father said. "Not that I can tell."

A terrible thought was forming in Taemon's head. What if his journal hadn't fallen out of his pocket after all? He recalled Vangie grabbing his journal from him, flipping through the pages with obvious interest. Staring at his drawing of the lock . . .

Taemon spoke up. "Did Vangie know about the—?" He stopped. Mr. Parvel was glaring intently at him. He realized that Vangie's parents were not supposed to know about the library.

"About the what?" Vangie's father asked.

Taemon hesitated. "About the pain she would cause everyone by leaving?" he finished lamely. Mr. Parvel relaxed slightly, and Vangie's mother burst into tears. Mrs. Parvel tried to comfort her, while Vangie's father started ranting about city life and the allure it held for impressionable young kids.

Taemon took advantage of the chaos to slip off his stool and whisper in Amma's ear: "Can I talk to you outside?"

"What?" Amma whispered. "You still have psi and you didn't tell me? How could you?"

"It's not *real* psi. Not the useful kind. And I was going to tell you. I just—"

Amma paced a few steps away, then turned and came back. "Let me get this straight. You actually drew pictures of the psi door and its lock? Holy Mother Mountain, Taemon! What were you thinking?"

He wished there was some way to explain why he'd done it. Nothing he could think of sounded logical. "It's just something that I—"

"My da's going to kill me. Then you. Skies, if I'd known you had psi, I never would have . . . My da's going to kill me."

"This is exactly why I didn't want to tell you," Taemon said. "I was afraid you'd treat me differently if you knew

I had psi. And I was right, wasn't I? You think of me completely differently now."

"That's not the point. You should have told me." Amma said. "Okay, let's think. Just because the journal is missing doesn't mean Vangie has it. And even if she does have it, maybe they'll find her before she shows it to anyone. Maybe it will be okay."

"Maybe. But we should still tell your da." Taemon tried to look her in the eye but she wouldn't meet his gaze. "Do you want me to go with you?"

"No," Amma said. "The library is my responsibility. Mine and my family's. And we'll honor it."

Taemon watched her walk back into the house.

After a miserable day and a restless night, Taemon had finally fallen asleep, only to be caught up in a nightmare. He was in the middle of an earthquake, and it wouldn't stop. He heard rumbling all around him. The ground trembled. He started awake, only to realize that the trembling wasn't part of a dream at all.

He threw on some clothes and ran in his bare feet through the tinker's shop and out the door. He saw Drigg standing in the street and stopped next to him.

"What is it? An earthquake?" Taemon asked.

"No. Haulers. Very large haulers," Drigg said, as if in a daze.

Half a dozen large vehicles were being driven into the colony. Much too large for the colony's small streets, they barreled over mailboxes, flowerbeds, bicycles—anything too close to the edge of the street.

"Why are they here? Are we being invaded?"

Drigg said nothing. He wouldn't even look at Taemon, but kept his eyes on the road.

"Shouldn't somebody do something?" Taemon said. He and Drigg were some of the only people on the street. Everyone else seemed to be hiding in their houses.

Drigg shook his head. "Do what? It would take an army to stop those haulers. We don't even have any authority officers."

The haulers were headed toward the square, away from the tinker's shop. Taemon turned back to get his shoes. "I have to find out what's going on."

Drigg grabbed his arm. "No, you don't. Best let them do what they came to do and get back to where they came from. Nothing you or I can do about it."

"You don't know that." Taemon yanked his arm free. "If it runs, don't fix it. Isn't that what you say? Well, something's broken. And maybe we can fix it."

Drigg took off his cap and rubbed his bald spot. "Blazes! A man can't argue with his own motto. C'mon. I'll go with you."

After putting their shoes on, they ran toward the square. The haulers had plowed right over the fountain, destroying the pipes and ripping up the concrete benches around it. Water spilled over gouged and scattered cobblestones, making it hard to run. By the time Taemon and Drigg caught up to them, the haulers had stopped. Apparently they'd reached their destination. Taemon craned his neck to see what lay beyond them.

Skies! They were lined up in front of Amma's house!

In an instant, dozens of temple guards were climbing out of the haulers. What the blazes was going on?

Out of the darkness, Hannova emerged. She was dressed in her nightclothes, her robe billowing out behind her. She strode up to a guard near the front. "You will explain this act of—?" As if a switch had been thrown, Hannova collapsed. Had they killed her?

"She is alive," said a voice that had been amplified with psi—a voice that Taemon would recognize anywhere. It was Elder Naseph. "But she will remain unconscious until we are finished here. We will not harm anyone who does not interfere with our mission. People of the colony, come forward! This is a historic occasion! We are here to claim this property in the name of the True Son, to benefit the New Cycle of Power! Your humble colony shall influence the course of history though its generous donation of knowledge!"

Skies! They were here for the library! Where was Amma and her family? He peered through the shadows, hoping to spot a familiar face.

Slowly, people made their way out of their houses and into the streets. Still, no one dared get too close to the large haulers or the fifty-odd burly temple guards surrounding Amma's house. The guards on the outside faced the crowd, watching for any sign of resistance. Taemon got as close as he dared, until he could see Elder Naseph. And beside him stood Yens.

A few guards burst out of the house, each one using psi to drag a prisoner with them. The Parvels. Their hands had been cuffed. The guards lined them up in front of the porch.

Elder Naseph turned to Yens. "Let's begin."

Yens nodded.

Five syringes came flying like darts from skies-knew-where. The serum. Each member of the Parvel family got stuck in the neck.

"Yes," said Yens, "we know your little secret. It won't change anything. Don't worry, I made sure you got a small dose. I want you to be conscious. So you can watch."

"You . . . have no right . . . to be here," Mr. Parvel said, his speech coming slowly, his body swaying. All of Amma's family looked like they were having trouble staying upright. "This property belongs to the colony."

"Not anymore," Yens said. "Brand-new cycle. Brand-new rules. Now, let's get busy."

He turned and stared at Amma's house. Suddenly the porch began ripping itself apart. Boards tore away from the frame. Shelves and all their ceramic contents crashed into piles of rubble. Cries and gasps came from the small crowd watching.

The piece-by-piece destruction of Amma's house

happened at an alarming rate. The stucco walls crumbed into dust. The wooden framework pulled itself apart. They were after the library. No doubt.

Furniture and linens and dishes and musical instruments flung themselves into the heaps of rubbish. Stuff, Taemon reminded himself. It was just stuff. As long as the psi door held. And he was sure it would.

The house was completely gone now, the rocky slope of the hillside lay bare under the morning sun. Mrs. Parvel's sobs echoed in the sudden silence. Only the psi door stood between Yens and the library. Yens grinned.

"You'll never . . . crack . . . the lock," said Mr. Parvel.

"We'll see," Yens said.

He wouldn't be able to do it. The lock was the most complicated thing Taemon had ever seen. And that door was solid. Taemon let his mind wander into the door just to assure himself that everything was in place. Yes, that door was tight as a —

Skies! The pins were beginning to drop inside the lock. Taemon stood stunned as one by one each wheel turned and each bolt retracted.

The door swung open.

Taemon ran forward. "Yens!"

One of the temple guards grabbed him and pinned him in place with psi. Yens turned around to face Taemon.

"I was hoping I'd get to see you on this trip. My dear younger brother."

Mr. Parvel gasped. "Brother?"

Amma groaned.

Her father turned with great effort to look at his daughter. "You . . . knew?"

She nodded. "I . . . never . . . thought . . . I'm so . . . sorry, Da."

Vangie. It had to be Vangie who had stolen his journal and taken it to the city. How it ended up in Yens's hands was anybody's guess.

Taemon tried to explain, but someone was holding his jaw shut with psi. He struggled against the psi that held him, but he could do nothing more than wriggle and murmur.

He watched the agony on Mr. Parvel's face as Yens strolled into the library.

The books started flying out of the door and into the haulers. Book after book. Stack after stack. A continuous stream of books disappeared into the haulers. And there was nothing anyone could do.

After a long, torturous half hour, Yens emerged from the cave that once held the library.

Elder Naseph, who had been content to let Yens do the dirty work until now, stepped forward and addressed the crowd. "Thank you so much for your donation to the cause. Now, we have one last order of business. One family here did not cooperate. That cannot go unpunished." He stared at the piles of rubble off to the side. Everything the Parvels owned lay in those heaps. Suddenly, flames erupted in each pile.

Elder Naseph turned his back on the destruction and climbed aboard one of the haulers. The burly temple guards all did the same. Yens had one foot on a hauler's running board when Challis showed up out of nowhere. "Do not go with these men, nephew," she said, looking directly at Yens. "They will betray you."

Yens stood perfectly still. Somehow Challis commanded his attention and no one moved to stop her. She grabbed hold of Yens's arm. Taemon saw him cringe, but, miraculously, he didn't pull away.

"I see things. I know what they're up to. Making psi weapons for the Republik. They're going to sell my nephew to the Republik right along with those weapons. That's a good way to get rid of him, isn't it? Sacrifice, they'll call it. The True Son sacrifices himself for the good of the true people." Challis shook a finger right in front of Yens's face. "Don't you do it!"

Yens paled.

Elder Naseph materialized. "Silence, woman!" Challis wilted and collapsed on the ground. He ordered Yens into the hauler, and in seconds they were rumbling off the way they had come.

With the haulers gone, the colonists jumped into action. There were flames to put out. People to care for. Drigg and Taemon hurried to check on the Parvels, who were sitting on the ground in a daze.

The cuffs had been unlocked, and the drugs were starting to wear off.

"Lost," Mr. Parvel mumbled. "Everything lost. How?"

"Let's get you all to the healer's," Drigg said. "Can you walk?"

Mr. Parvel ignored Drigg and focused on Taemon. "It was you, wasn't it? You helped him—helped him steal from us. I just can't figure out how."

"I'm so sorry. It was an accident."

"An accident? An *accident*?" Mr. Parvel stood up on wobbly legs.

Drigg braced his shoulder underneath Mr. Parvel's arm and started leading him away. "We'll work through all that later, Birch. Let's get you and yours to the healer."

Taemon turned to Amma. "I'm so sorry."

She looked at him blankly. "Sorry changes nothing."

16 REED

Flower fades as Reed grows tall.

Reed, the dreamer of them all,

Considers every point of view,

Deeply ponders what to do.

His thoughts are big, his actions small.

His thoughts are big, his actions small.

— CALENDAR SONG

Hours later, when Hannova, Challis, and the Parvels had recovered, Taemon had been summoned to a council meeting to explain himself. After he told the council what he thought had happened, not everyone was convinced.

"He didn't do anything wrong," Drigg said. "He told you what happened. That Vangie girl stole his journal."

"But how do we know he's telling the truth?" Mr. Parvel said.

"I vouch for him," said Drigg. "Hannova does, too. Challis backs him up. Skies, what more do you want?"

"I want the library back!" Mr. Parvel thundered.

Hannova spoke next. "The library is a terrible loss, no doubt about it. But what's done is done. We have to look forward. Challis, what about this war you say is coming? Is there any chance it can be prevented?"

"There is one chance," said Challis. "He's sitting right over there." She nodded toward Taemon.

"Him?" Mr. Parvel sputtered. "He's the one who started it!"

Taemon's face burned, but he could hardly argue with that. If he hadn't let his mind wander into that psi door, if he hadn't felt the need to draw what he'd seen in his journal, if he hadn't left his journal where Vangie could find it, then none of this would be happening.

Challis frowned at Mr. Parvel. "It was always going to happen that way. No use blaming the boy for doing what he'd already done."

Mr. Parvel and a few others grumbled, but no one challenged her point. Finally, Taemon worked up the courage to ask the obvious question: "How am I supposed to stop the war?"

"You're not going to like it," Challis said.

He wasn't surprised to hear that. Was putting a stop to a war ever enjoyable? "If there's a way that I can undo what I've done, I'll try. Just tell me what I have to do."

"You'll have to go back to the city," Challis said.

She was right. He didn't like it.

"Go back to the city? And do what, exactly? Steal back the books? What if they've read some of them by now? They'll know how to do all sorts of things—horrible things," he said, shuddering as he remembered what Mr. Parvel had told him about atoms. "What can I possibly do to stop them?"

"I can't tell you exactly," Challis said. "I haven't seen how things turn out. But one thing's clear. You have to keep Yens from going to the Republik. Make him part ways with the high priest. If he keeps following Naseph's orders, there'll be no stopping the war."

Taemon leaned forward in his seat. "You're telling me I have to convince Yens to step down from being the True Son."

Challis nodded.

He shook his head. "That's . . . impossible."

"One more thing," Challis said, ignoring him entirely. "The Water girl has to go with you."

"Now, wait one minute," Mr. Parvel said, but Hannova shushed him.

"We have a chance to divert a war," said Hannova. "Even if it's an incredibly small chance, we have to take it."

A quick vote proved that this was the general consensus of the council. There was no arguing with a seer. If Taemon and Amma were their best shot at avoiding war, then back to the city they would go.

Taemon just wished it were someone else they were all depending on.

They would take the byrider. Drigg had reinstalled the original psi motor, and it was running fine. Taemon gave Amma a very unthorough driving lesson, and Challis gave Taemon a bag of food and a hug. Challis had told them they didn't have much time, so they set out on the shortest route, which would put them at the West Gate in about two hours.

Taemon sat behind Amma on the byrider. Holding on to her waist gave him a weird feeling. Not bad, just weird. Adding to the weirdness were the psi clothes he was wearing, the same clothes he'd worn in the city on his birthday; they felt more uncomfortable than ever.

They got off to a rough start. It took a while before Amma could run the byrider's engine at a constant speed and steer at the same time. She was getting better as they went, but she tired quickly, which meant they had to stop frequently. Taemon wished he could talk to her, bounce around some ideas about what to do once they got to the city. But he knew she needed to focus on driving.

About an hour into the drive, they had yet to see another vehicle. Tall spindly pine trees lined the paved road. A bald eagle swooped down on the left and settled on a tree to watch them go by.

"Did you see that?" Amma asked. "The Eagle is a good sign for us right now. It means we're going to succeed."

Taemon grunted. The other meaning for Eagle was isolation. That was probably the more likely outcome.

The byrider started veering to the left.

"Don't look at the bird." Taemon said.

"Why?"

"Where you look is where you go," he said. "That's the first rule of driving with psi. If you don't want to go there, don't look at it."

"Got it," she said. The byrider's path straightened out.

When they crossed a bridge over a small stream, Taemon noticed the reeds growing along its banks. Reed was a better sign for them right now than Eagle. Reed was all about thinking, and that's what Taemon needed to do. Think. Think of a plan.

Skies, he did *not* want to go to the city! What would they do there? How could they stop Yens? Even with Amma's psi, the task seemed impossible. They were outnumbered, outpowered, and outsmarted.

The byrider began weaving in the road.

"Need a rest?" Taemon said.

"Nah," said Amma. "We'd better keep going."

They swerved onto the shoulder of the road, kicking up rocks and narrowly missing a ditch.

"Not if you keep driving like that. We'd better take a break."

"Maybe you're right." Amma cut off power to the engine, and they slowed to a stop. They led the bike across a shallow part of the ditch, then found a shady spot and sat down. Taemon pulled some salted meat out of the sack, broke it, and handed half to Amma.

"Is it my imagination, or does using psi make you hungry?" she asked.

"It used to make me hungry," said Taemon. "But I'm always hungry."

"I can't believe how much concentration that takes. How do people do it all day every day?"

Taemon shrugged. "You get used to it. After a while you don't have to think about it so much. When I first lost my psi, I kept forgetting it wasn't there anymore. Kept trying to use it, you know, to open doors, turn on lights, get dressed."

Heat rose from his neck to his face. What was he thinking, talking about getting dressed? He was so stupid when it came to talking to girls. He turned his head and ripped off another bite of the tough salted meat.

Amma cleared her throat. "So, when we get to Deliverance, what do we do first?"

"We'll find my parents. They might be able to tell us something about Yens." And even if they couldn't, Taemon would feel a whole lot better knowing they were okay. "After that, I don't know." He stared down at the ground. "This is hopeless."

"Hey." Amma touched his arm. He looked up at her. "Where you look is where you go, remember? Don't look at hopeless. We don't want to go there."

"What else is there to look at?"

"Form an image in your mind of what you want to happen, then do what it takes to make it happen. It's just like using psi."

"Only I have no way to make it happen," Taemon muttered.

Amma frowned. "If that's what you think, then why did you come?"

"Challis said I had to." Taemon shrugged. "Besides, what other choice do I have? Sit around and wait for the war to start?"

Amma stood up. "We have lots of choices right now, Taemon. About a million."

"Name one."

"Running away."

"Where? We can't go back to the colony. We can't live in Deliverance."

"So? There are other cities. We have a byrider. We have a couple days' food. We could go anywhere. We could go to the Republik."

Taemon scrunched his brow. "How would we get there? Drigg said no one can cross the mountains."

"There's got to be a way. We could do it. Why not?" Amma threw one hand up in the air and let it fall.

Was she serious? She looked serious. If they went to the Republik, they wouldn't have anywhere to go, wouldn't know anyone who would help them. But how was that different than what awaited them in Deliverance? Maybe she had a point.

Except that it felt completely wrong.

He shook his head. "We should at least try."

Amma knelt down and looked Taemon in the eye. "Why? Why should we try?"

Taemon leaned back. Sometimes Amma was one intense girl. "Um . . . because we said we would?"

"So what? We can change our minds, can't we? Because it's hopeless, right?"

Now she was getting downright annoying. Taemon began packing the food and water back into the sack. "We shouldn't argue right now. We have to at least try to stop this war. We're not running away, so let's just get going."

Amma sat back on her heels and crossed her arms. "I'm not budging until I know why you're doing this. And I'm the driver, remember?"

Taemon glared at Amma. What did she want him to say? She could be so infuriating. They were wasting time. He threw the sack to the ground. "Look, we're doing this because it's the right thing to do. Those flaming priests got their hands on those books, and they're making weapons. If there's even a chance of us stopping a war, we have to try."

Amma picked up the sack and patted Taemon on the head. "Good. Now we can go."

He followed her to the byrider and wondered what went on in that girl's head. Or any girl's head, for that matter.

An hour later, Taemon figured they must be a couple of miles from the city wall. He tapped Amma's shoulder. "Let's stop here. We need to talk before we go any farther."

Amma nodded and brought the byrider to a stop. They both hopped off, and Amma grabbed the handlebars to lead the byrider into the trees by the side of the road.

"Not like that," Taemon said. "Use psi."

Amma nodded and let go of the byrider. It wheeled itself toward the trees while the two of them walked behind it.

They sat down in the shade of the trees. "Now it gets

tricky," he whispered. "You'll have to use psi for both of us from now on."

"I know how to use psi," Amma said. "I've had it all my life."

"I'm still getting used to that idea. You did a good job of hiding it."

She smiled. "I thought for sure you would figure it out from the earthquake. Remember? When I moved that rock out of the way?"

"That was you?" Taemon stared in disbelief. "Still, you're not used to doing everyday things with psi. When we're in the city, you can't forget and use your hands."

Amma nodded.

"Okay," he said. "Now take the backpack off my shoulders, and I'll pretend I'm doing it." Taemon felt the straps yank his arms backward. "Slow down!"

Amma took a deep breath. This time the backpack eased itself off his back and floated to the ground.

"Much better. Take the water bottle out and remove the lid."

"You can't keep telling me every little thing," Amma said. "I'm pretty sure I can figure out how to get a drink of water."

She drew the water out of the bottle and toward her mouth. She gulped. "See? I did it."

"Good," Taemon said. "Now some water for me."

"You got it," she said. Another glob of water floated out of the bottle and toward Taemon. He opened his mouth and sucked it in. The last few drops splashed up his nose and made him cough.

Amma laughed.

"Hey, no flubbing around."

"Sorry," Amma said. "Couldn't resist."

Taemon pulled out paper and a pencil from the sack they'd brought along. He drew a diagram of what a simple light switch looked like inside a wall.

"All light switches are identical so that everyone knows what to envision when using psi to turn a light on and off. That makes it so that anyone can flip any switch. Slide the metal up, and the circuit is complete, which makes electricity flow to the light and turn it on. Slide it down, and the circuit is broken, which makes the light turn off."

Amma nodded. "So all switches look like this?"

"Yep," Taemon said. "Unless for some reason you don't want anybody else flipping your switch. Then you can make it different, and only you know what it looks like.

Now let's talk about doors. Do you know what a standard door latch looks like?"

"No," Amma said.

He drew another diagram, this time of a common door latch.

"Same principle works for doors. If you want anybody to be able to open a door, you have a regular latch that looks like this. Very simple. Anybody can lift this little lever here and open the door."

"Anybody with psi," Amma said.

What a pair we are, thought Taemon. Amma had the power but no knowledge. Taemon had knowledge but no power. Amma couldn't share her power, but Taemon could share his knowledge. Some if it, anyway. Sharing knowledge was not a quick thing, and Taemon wasn't sure if his drawings were good enough for Amma to picture things in her head perfectly. When he'd learned about light switches in school, they'd been able to look at an actual switch.

Taemon covered a few more topics like water faucets, seat belts, and how to flush a toilet. Now all they needed was a way to get past the gate guards and into the city.

"Do you have any ideas?" Amma asked. "You know more about the gate guards than I do."

An idea *had* been forming in Taemon's mind. He nodded. "Are you up for a little frivolics?"

Amma smiled. "Always."

Half an hour later, they caught sight of the city wall. Having ditched the byrider in the woods, they walked on foot through the trees, behind a cluster of pines, and near enough for a good look at the gate.

"There it is," said Taemon. "The West Gate."

Amma squinted. "I can only see two guards. This frivolics idea just might work. Are we ready?"

Taemon pulled his hat down as much as he dared. "Ready."

The two of them burst out of the woods, laughing and running for the West Gate.

"Beat you!" said Amma when she reached the guards first. "Now you can't stop me from asking."

The guards looked curiously at Amma. Taemon raced up behind her, then stopped and traced one foot in the dirt, looking down at it as though he were embarrassed.

"You don't have to ask them," Taemon said. "I'll tell the truth this time."

"No," Amma teased. "I'm not sure I believe you anymore. I'll ask these fine, trustworthy gate guards. They'll tell me the truth."

"Tell you the truth about what?" one guard asked.

"Are those woods really full of bears?" She pointed toward the woods they'd just left.

The guards laughed heartily. "A hundred years ago, maybe."

"I knew it." Amma stamped her foot. "I knew it wasn't true. We went for a hike from the North Gate to the West Gate. And this . . . this scoundrel told me tales about bears just to scare me."

Taemon tried to look embarrassed, turning his face away from the guard and looking at the ground.

The guard snorted. "Go easy on the boy. He just wanted you to hold his hand."

The other guard was more serious. "You kids oughtn't be hiking around here. Might not be safe. Go home, now, and stay out of trouble."

Amma harrumphed. "My thoughts exactly. I can think

of better ways to win a girl's heart than scaring her half to death." She stomped through the gate, chin lifted.

Taemon hurried after her. "Aww, don't be mad! I was just having a bit of fun!"

The guards were still laughing as Taemon and Amma passed through the gate unchallenged.

They came to an intersection and turned a corner. Taemon glanced around, then whispered, "Perfect performance."

"Thank you," Amma said, looking around with wide eyes. Taemon followed her stare. Shacks leaned up against the city wall. Raggedy-looking children played in the dirt. Skinny stray cats roamed the area. An old lady struggled with a deep cough. Taemon fought the urge to hold his nose; it smelled like fermented beans around here.

He'd only been gone three months. How had the city declined so quickly? He had to find out what was going on. It was time to find his parents.

Twenty minutes later, Taemon showed Amma the place he thought he'd never see again: his home.

But he almost didn't recognize it when he saw it. The grass was dead. The windows were boarded up. And it wasn't just his house. There were plenty of others that looked the same. What in the Great Green Earth was going on? He led Amma up the front steps.

He stared at the front door. Now what?

"Well?" Amma said.

"I can't unlock the door," Taemon whispered. "And neither can you. Skies, we can't even ring the doorbell." Even if he could tell her how these things worked, she wouldn't be able to operate them without seeing them for herself. They were doomed if they couldn't do even the simplest things.

Amma reached out and knocked.

Taemon looked around, hoping no one had seen what she'd just done.

"Relax," Amma said. "There's no one around."

"Go away!" came a gruff voice from behind the door. Was that Da? "This house is occupied."

"It's Taemon," he said, as loudly as he dared.

Taemon heard the latch click and the door swung open.

"Get in here," the voice said. "Hurry!"

Taemon and Amma stepped inside into a dim living room. When Taemon's eyes adjusted, he saw his uncle Fierre staring back at him.

"Taemon! Skies above, it is you!" Uncle Fierre looked thin and gaunt, his eyes bloodshot, his face stubbly. "I thought they shipped you off to the dud farm. Was that a lie?"

"It's true. I was at the colony, but I came back to help. Are you okay? Where's Mam and Da?"

"I'd ask you to sit down, but as you can see, there's nowhere to sit. Are you hungry? I might have some food. Somewhere. Or maybe it's gone. I forget."

Taemon looked around and realized that the furniture was gone. "What's happened?"

"Don't believe I've had the pleasure, Miss," Uncle Fierre said to Amma. She introduced herself, and then Uncle Fierre took a deep breath and rubbed the whiskers on his chin. "Blazes, I don't even know where to start. I'm so tired I can't think."

"When's the last time you slept, Uncle Fierre?" Taemon asked.

"When's the last time you ate?" added Amma.

Uncle Fierre dismissed their concerns with a wave of his hand. "You know your father: he just couldn't keep his mouth shut. He was one of the first they took away.

So many people are missing. It's chaos. I have to keep the squatters away."

Taemon's thoughts spun. They'd taken his da? Had they taken Mam, too? Where were they? Were they okay? But the question that came out was: "Squatters?"

"Cha," Amma said. "We saw a lot of those when we came in through the West Gate."

Uncle Fierre shrugged. "Desperate times. So many houses destroyed. So many people left homeless. Senseless. Wasteful. People see an empty house, and they figure nobody's coming back to claim it."

Taemon took a step back. "What do you mean nobody's coming back? Where are they?"

Fierre shook his head. "At the asylums, maybe? Prisons? There are rumors flying everywhere. No one knows anything."

"Have you heard anything about Taemon's brother? Or the war?" Amma asked.

"War, yes. War. The priests are preparing everyone. They say sacrifices must be made."

"I don't understand," Taemon said. "Who is the war against?"

Uncle Fierre sat on the floor and hung his head. "We're lucky this house is still standing. War. Squatters. They're everywhere. Sacrifices. Ha!"

His uncle laughed—at least Taemon thought it was laughter—long and loud, then stopped abruptly. "Have you seen your da? Tell him I'm keeping the squatters away. Are you hungry? Skies, I'm tired."

Amma turned to Taemon. "We should let him sleep." She touched his shoulder. "I'm so sorry about your parents."

Taemon nodded. He wanted to feel sorry, too, but feeling sorry wasn't going to help anyone. "We'll have to see what we can find out on our own."

They left Uncle Fierre a little food from their pack and moved on.

Amma and Taemon hid behind some azaleas in Moke's backyard to wait and see if the plan worked. Taemon had found a stray psiball in his friend's yard, and Amma had used her psi to wedge it between the tree limbs. It was their old signal that psiball practice was on. Psiball was the only fun thing he could remember from those fearful days after he'd lost his psi. They'd had fun, hadn't they? He and Moke? Until that ugly scene at the tournament.

In a few minutes, Moke came out to the backyard with a quizzical look on his face. "Taemon?" he whispered.

Taemon stepped from the bushes. "Hoy, Moke." Without warning, strong emotions welled up inside Taemon. He reached out to hug his old psiball partner.

Moke stiffened and stepped back. "What are you doing? Why are you here? Do you have any idea what could happen if—" Moke's eyebrows arched high as he looked at something behind Taemon's shoulder.

Taemon turned and saw Amma stepping out of the azaleas.

"Are there more of you?" Moke asked. "Is this an invasion?"

"Just the two of us," Taemon said. "Amma, this is Moke. His parents run the crematorium. He studies weasel droppings. He makes sculptures out of cat hair. And he . . ." Taemon couldn't bring himself to say what came next.

"And I stink at picking a psiball partner," Moke said with a wry smile. Taemon returned the smile, but he still couldn't read Moke's mood.

"Crematorium?" Amma's question broke the awkward silence. "Is that like an ice-cream store?"

Moke and Taemon burst out laughing, which erased all

the tension. Despite Amma's demands, neither boy could bring himself to tell her the truth.

"Seriously," Taemon said at last, turning to Moke. "I'm sorry about the tournament. I thought I could keep it a secret. I was stupid."

Moke shook his head. "It's ancient history. I just wish you had told me." Moke turned to Amma. "This guy really knows how to stir things up."

"How'd you like to help us do some serious stirring?" Taemon asked.

Moke listened patiently as Taemon and Amma explained about the library, about the high priest's deal with the Republik and their planned double cross, and about how Yens was the key to stopping the war.

"This explains a lot," said Moke. "Last Sabbath the priests kept talking about restoring lost knowledge and the True Son humbling the heathen nations. They're trying to get everybody thinking it's time to take our rightful place in the world. Everyone's talking about psi weapons." He frowned. "What I don't get is how the library fits into the high priest's plans. They were already building their weapons before they attacked the colony."

"I'm not sure either," said Taemon. "But it must have

something to do with the Republik. Maybe the library gives the priests a stronger position. Something else to bargain with."

Amma balled her hands into fists. "If everyone knows about the weapons, why doesn't anyone do anything?"

"Anyone who speaks out is gone the next day." Moke frowned. "But the priests never actually use the word *war.* They make it sound like everyone else will just give up because they'll see how powerful we are."

"They might be right about that," Taemon said. Silence fell among the three of them for a moment.

"Is there any way you can get us inside the temple?" Taemon asked. "I have to get to Yens somehow—without the priests knowing."

"No," Moke said. "But I might know someone who can help." His expression was determined. "Meet me back here just before dark." Moke opened the gate with psi and hurried off.

"Are you sure we can trust him?" Amma said.

"Skies, I hope so."

17 TURTLE

Reed's day is through when Turtle shows.

Turtle sticks to what he knows.

He thinks ahead and plans his day,

And from that plan he hates to stray.

He does not care if he is slow.

He does not care if he is slow.

— CALENDAR SONG

"How long till sundown?" Taemon asked Amma. "Two hours? Three?"

"Closer to two, I'd say," Amma replied.

"I think we should stay put," said Amma at exactly the same moment that Taemon said, "Let's go into the city."

Amma looked at Taemon incredulously. "What if you're recognized? Or what if I do something wrong, something that gets us noticed? People are scared. Haven't you picked up on that? Who knows what they'll do if something spooks them."

"We can't pin all our hopes on Moke," Taemon said, rubbing the back of his neck. "If we go into the city, we might learn something that would help us. We could get a feel for what people are thinking, what they're saying. Maybe it will help us think of a plan."

"We'll have to avoid attention." Amma frowned, turning her head and looking at him sideways. "Are you *sure* it's worth the risk?"

"You can stay here if you want," Taemon said. "I . . . I have to go out there. I can't play it safe anymore and hope for the best. Maybe it won't be enough. Maybe it won't matter. But if we fail, I want to know I did everything I could think of."

Amma nodded. "Fair enough."

Taemon tipped the brim of his hat to hide his eyes, and the two of them walked toward the city.

"If it's gossip we're after, we should go to the plaza," Taemon said. "It used to be crowded this time of day, but we'll see."

"Whatever you say," Amma said.

On the short walk to the plaza, Taemon realized just how much the city had changed. On a beautiful spring day like this, he should see people trimming their hedges, kids riding scooters, playing psiball. Hardly anyone was out. Maybe there would be more activity at the plaza.

They came to a crossroads. Amma glanced around, then nodded toward a sign with the Turtle symbol. "What's that for?" she asked furtively.

"That's a street sign," Taemon said, directing her to the right. "Wrong way. We're not taking Turtle Street."

Amma shook her head in disgust. "I can't believe people don't read."

Taemon shushed her, and they walked the rest of the way in silence. The plaza was close now, and they were starting to see a few people here and there. He couldn't risk anyone overhearing them.

Taemon detected delicious smells in the air and directed Amma to the eating area, a large open space with tables and chairs.

Amazingly, there were even a few food carts out. People still had to eat, he supposed. Amma stopped at a pastry vendor's cart. "Ooh, that orange one looks good. Can we get one of those for dessert?"

Taemon directed her away from the pastry cart. "That thing is so spicy, it could digest your stomach instead of the other way around."

"Okay," said Amma. "What do you suggest?"

Taemon caught a whiff of the most heavenly food on the Great Green Earth. "Lamb rolls!"

He found the lamb roll vendor and ordered two portions. Amma used psi to take the money out of their sack and give it to the vendor, all while making it look like it was Taemon who was doing it.

"Nice job," Taemon whispered as they made their way to the dining area. There were plenty of seats for them to choose from, but Taemon steered them toward an empty table near a small group of townspeople.

Amma made a little bow. "Thank you. Let's eat."

Using psi, she broke off a piece of lamb roll and floated it into her mouth. "Mmm. These are delicious." She took another bite.

Taemon's belly growled. He hoped he wouldn't have to remind her that she had to use psi for both of them. He was dying to get a taste of that lamb roll.

"Oh, wow. Is that sage I'm tasting?" She took two more bites. "And that dough they roll it in. Skies, that's good!"

"Cha," said Taemon. "It's wonderful."

"Oh . . . sorry." Amma broke off a small piece of Taemon's lamb roll and floated it toward his mouth. He closed his eyes and let the flavor seep into his tongue. It was every bit as good as he remembered.

"I think I'll take another bite," Taemon hinted.

Amma held up her finger to motion for Taemon to wait. "Listen," she whispered.

"I don't know what you're worried about," said a man sitting a couple tables over. "The Republik wants to be our ally."

"But what if that changes?" a woman said. "Can we trust them?"

"They're powerless. We'll have the upper hand no matter what."

"But Solovar says different."

"And look where that landed him! On the run from the authority officers. His wife taken away."

The conversation lulled uncomfortably for a moment.

"So, do you think we'll get any psiball games this season? The Aqua team has to defend its title."

"It's starting to get dark," said Amma. She rose from her chair. "We'd better go."

Taemon stayed in his chair and looked at his barely nibbled lamb roll. "I'm not done yet."

Amma rolled her eyes. "Oh, for Skies' sake." She quickly

broke the lamb roll into four large bites and floated them all at once toward Taemon's mouth. When he snatched them with his mouth, he could hardly fit them all in.

Moke was waiting for them in his backyard. "Where were you?" he asked. "I was starting to think you'd gotten caught!" His face looked a little pale.

"Sorry. We wanted to check out the plaza, see if we could overhear anything useful. Hey, have you heard of a person named Solovar?"

Moke nodded. "He used to be president of the trade guild association."

"Used to be?" asked Taemon.

"Cha, used to be. Until he spoke out against the high priest, lost his job, and went into hiding. Now he's kind of an underground leader for people who don't like Elder Naseph."

"He sounds perfect," Taemon said. "Do you think he would help us?"

"Maybe," Moke said. "But like I said, he's in hiding. No one would tell me how to contact him. I tried to spread the word about our meeting; maybe he'll hear about it and show up."

"So you set up a meeting?" Amma said.

Moke nodded. "At an empty warehouse down by the West Wall. It's used as a gambling salon now. I'm not sure how many people will actually come to talk to you, but it was the best I could do."

Amma looked surprised. "Gambling is legal here?"

"No," Taemon said. "At least it wasn't when I left."

Amma raised her eyebrows and formed her lips into a silent "Oh."

The West Wall. Where the shacks were. It made sense. Where else would they find people who weren't afraid of going against authority? The people there had little to lose.

"Well, let's get going," Taemon said.

Minutes later, Taemon and Amma followed Moke through a narrow space in front of a row of wall shanties. Taemon wondered if people had to use psi to keep their houses from collapsing.

They turned down a dusty alley. Fading light from the sunset made the swirling dust look gray like fog. Picking his way around garbage and a delivery hauler missing its wheels, Moke led them to the warehouse, then used psi to open the sliding door.

Taemon took a few steps inside the door and stopped. It was too dark to see anything. Once again, he couldn't turn on the lights without psi. It was so incredibly annoying. "Will someone please turn on the lights?" he whispered.

"I'm trying," Amma said, stepping into the doorway beside him. "It's not working."

"Just go in!" Moke's voice cracked with nervous tension. "We don't want anyone to see us standing around."

Taemon shuffled forward a few steps, but felt a strong reluctance to go any farther into that dark room despite Moke's urging.

"Is it empty?" Amma asked, her voice echoing. "No one showed?"

"Not completely empty."

An authority officer stepped from the shadows, dressed in black and floating two pairs of psi cuffs in front of him. The lights switched on. Three other officers came into view behind him. "You're under arrest for insubordination."

Taemon felt his arms being pulled behind his back. Why hadn't he thought to use clairvoyance before he'd walked into the trap? Skies, it was the one thing he could do and he hadn't even thought of it! How useless could he get?

He looked at Amma. Her arms were pinned behind her back, too. The psi cuffs drifted toward them and fastened over their wrists. The cuffs were made of a thick metal, too strong to break even with psi and secured with a complicated lock that probably only the arresting officer knew how to release.

"Moke turned us in!" Amma's shoulder muscles tensed and she grunted with the effort. She was struggling against the strong psi that held her in place.

"Do not resist," the officer said.

Taemon tried to look over his shoulder to see if Moke was still behind him. He couldn't turn his head very far, but in the corner of his vision, he saw Moke walking away with the authorities. Taemon knew he should be angry, but he felt only sadness. Moke must have been furious over the psiball tournament after all. This was his way of repaying Taemon for that humiliating day.

Amma yelled, "Add yourself to that weasel dung collection of yours, Moke!"

"Put them in the hauler with the others," the head officer said.

Taemon and Amma were turned around roughly with psi and shoved through the open door. Taemon's upper body was being pushed forward, and it was up to him to make his legs keep up or stumble face-first into the dirt. He was amazed that he and Amma made it to the hauler without falling.

They staggered into the back of the hauler, which was nearly full with a dozen or so people sitting inside it.

Taemon took a seat next to a man with white stubble on his chin and a weary look on his face. The hauler's engine started, and they lurched forward.

"You the kids from the colony?" the man next to Taemon asked, his voice low and gruff.

Taemon nodded.

"We heard about you. Came to hear what you had to say. But the offies got there first and arrested everybody."

"Moke ratted on us," Amma spat.

Taemon grunted. He was surprised that Moke had actually set up the meeting. If he was just going to turn them in, why bother getting others to show up? Maybe there was a reward for each arrest.

"Young Moke?" someone else said. "Why would he do that?"

Taemon sighed. "It's a long story."

A woman leaned forward and whispered to Taemon, "Is it true what young Moke said? Did the high priest discover a library in the powerless colony?"

Taemon nodded. "I'm afraid so."

"I have a brother there," the woman said. "He got word to me about what happened. Said the True Son destroyed an entire building, nearly killed the family that lived there."

"That family was lucky," Amma said, her voice strained. "They still have each other. But if the high priest goes through with his war, lots of people will die."

"People will die if we go against the high priest, too," someone mumbled.

"Maybe so," Taemon said. "But thousands of people die in a war. Maybe hundreds of thousands. We can't let that happen. It's not right for people with psi to use it for violence. Isn't that why the powerless colony was established in the first place? Because being powerless makes you vulnerable?"

The hauler came to a stop. The prisoners stopped talking while the hauler idled.

"Destination?" a voice said from outside. It must be a gate guard.

"Power plant," the driver said.

"Proceed."

The power plant. Taemon should have guessed. The power plant was also the jail where prisoners were forced to use their psi to turn the big turbines that made electricity for the city.

When the hauler moved forward again, the white-whiskered man lifted his head. "We're not so fond of the high priest ourselves. Or that cocky True Son. But what are we supposed to do? If you've got a plan that'll work, you can count on us to help."

The other people in the hauler murmured their agreement.

"I need to talk to Yens," Taemon said.

"The True Son? He doesn't talk to anybody. Hardly ever leaves the temple."

"Can anyone here get me into the temple?" he asked. He held his breath. What would he do if they all said no? If he couldn't get to Yens in time, how was he supposed to stop—?

"I can," the white-whiskered man said. "One of the temple guards is our man. But even if we get you in there, what makes you think he'll listen?"

"He's my brother. I think he'll at least let me talk to him."

Someone scoffed. "Cha. Right before he kills you."

"Here's the thing," Amma said. "We have reason to believe that if Taemon can get in to talk to his brother, we have a chance at stopping the war. There is a woman in the colony, Challis. She's a seer. She knows things that no one else does. And she says we have to get Taemon in to see Yens if we want to stop the war."

The other prisoners in the hauler didn't seem convinced.

"I don't know. . . ."

"Why should we trust someone we've never met?"

"Seems hopeless."

"Anybody else here have a better idea?" The bearded man spoke in a commanding voice. "We're going to the power plant one way or the other. With a plan or without a plan. I say this boy's plan is worth trying. They came all the way from the colony, for Skies' sake. That shows gumption."

His words silenced the others.

"If you can get me into the temple, I can try to persuade Yens against going to war," Taemon said. "But first we're going to have to escape from the power plant. Can anyone here describe the turbines inside the plant? Is there a way to dismantle them?"

Luckily, the old man had been locked up before. Taemon pressed him for details, then leaned forward and began putting together a plan.

18 JAGUAR

Turtle knows he must fall back
When Jaguar leaps in to attack.
A flash of teeth, a noisy fray,
That's how Jaguar rules his day.
His confidence will never crack.
His confidence will never crack.

— CALENDAR SONG

"Everybody out!" the head authority officer yelled.

Taemon jumped out first. He felt sorry for the older prisoners, who had a hard time getting out of the hauler with their hands cuffed behind their backs.

They were marched into an industrial-looking building with metal walls and doors and turned over to the prison guards.

"Well, well," one of the guards said. "Look who's back."

Panic flashed through Taemon's mind. Did they know who he was?

The guard grinned at the white-whiskered man. "Solovar's come to pay us another visit."

So, the old man was Solovar. Taemon turned to Amma. "Interesting," he whispered.

"No talking!" said a guard.

The guards crammed the prisoners into an open-air elevator. Taemon peeked over the edge, but all he saw was darkness below him. He wondered how far down it went. This time he thought to use clairvoyance; the elevator shaft went down deep. Deeper even than the lowest level of the building. It must have been made from an old well, because the bottom of the shaft was filled with water.

"Keep your flaming head inside the elevator," the guard said. "I hate it when I have to clean up blood."

Taemon shuffled away from the edge. "It sure looks like a big drop!" he said. He kept his tone light for the sake of the guards, but he hoped his fellow prisoners understood the significance of his observation.

The elevator took them down. When the door opened, the guards herded them through a hallway and into a grimy room with no furniture. Rust marks streaked from the ceiling. It smelled like corn fuel. And it was hot.

A man in dirty blue coveralls was waiting for them. He

looked over the new batch of prisoners. "Fourteen of you, huh? Good. Now we have enough grunts to run all four turbines on the night shift."

One of the guards came forward to speak to the coveralls man.

"Sir, two of these prisoners are from the dud farm and likely powerless. We have reason to believe the high priest has some interest in them, though. We've sent a runner to the temple for further instructions."

Coveralls man waved a dismissive hand at the guard. "I don't give a fig. If the high priest wants 'em, he'll have to come and get 'em. There's big doings at the temple tomorrow, and it's my head if the electricity runs out. We got one rule in this place: prisoners turn the turbines. If any of these grunts are powerless, the others will have to work that much harder." He smiled and showed his stained teeth.

Four more coveralls-clad people, two men and two women, came in. One of the guards removed the psi cuffs, passed each prisoner a dingy yellow jumpsuit, and told them to put it on over their clothes—with their hands.

The other prisoners grumbled at the unnecessary

humiliation, but for Taemon, the one without psi, it was a lucky break. He and Amma did as they were told. Their escape plan wouldn't work if they didn't make it into the turbine room, so they had to cooperate at least until that point.

"What about the zipper?" one of the prisoners asked. "We need to use our psi for that."

Taemon studied the fasteners on the jumpsuit. The prisoner was right; they would need to use psi to zip them up. Skies! Why hadn't he thought to teach Amma about clothing fasteners? She wouldn't be able to zip her jumpsuit either. They'd be forced to ask one of the guards to zip it for them. Well, he wasn't going to ask. He let the suit hang open in the front. Who flaming cared?

Taemon looked around and noticed that everyone seemed to be staring at their zippers and frowning.

"I think my zipper's broken," one woman said.

"Mine too," said someone else.

One of the guards rolled her eyes. "Attention, idiots. We don't use regular zippers in prison. Only the guards know how to zip up the suits. That's so you can't take them off whenever you want."

Another guard snickered. "And you're going to want. Cha, you will."

Taemon felt the zipper fasten itself and the jumpsuit become snug around his chest.

Next they were led back to the elevator, which took them deeper into the power plant. When the elevator stopped, Taemon got his first look at the turbine room.

It was just as Solovar had described it: The room was about three stories high. Four big turbines stood like a row of huge tree trunks in the center of the room. Each turbine column looked to be about five feet in diameter. Five small prison cells had been built around each turbine like petals around a stem. A yellow-jumpsuited prisoner stood in each cell, watching the facing turbine column and using psi to turn it.

The guard took Taemon's group of prisoners across a narrow platform that went along the edges of the room halfway between the floor and the ceiling. "Get a good look at the turbines," said the guard. "It's not that hard to see how they work. In a couple minutes, you're going to be down there turning them."

Taemon felt a pinch on his shoulder. "Pay attention!" said the guard. "I'm explaining how to do this. You stay in your cell and look at the turbine column in front of you. Use your psi to turn that column to the right. See them vertical stripes painted on the column? When those stripes are moving from the left to the right, it means the turbine is turning and we're making electricity. We watch those stripes to see how fast you're turning the turbine. Any questions?"

Taemon cleared his throat.

"You got a question?"

"You explained the stripes on the turbine column," Taemon said. "But what are the circles at the top?" He was pretty sure he knew what the fist-size circles high above the stripes were, but he wanted to be sure the others knew, too.

"Those aren't circles, idiot. They're screws. The turbine has to connect to the generator shaft somehow, don't it?" The guard shook his head. "Never mind. You grunts have no idea how this thing works. Just forget about the circles. They're not important."

Taemon looked at the other prisoners. This was the

plan they'd discussed in the hauler. Take the screws out without the guards noticing. Then the turbines would shut down, and that's when they'd make a break for it.

The guard was still talking. "Now, so you don't think this is a resort of some kind and not a prison, I'm telling you that if one of us guards sees them stripes aren't turning fast enough, we will provide you with a little incentive."

Taemon felt something sharp gouge his back. He flinched. Skies! What was that? He looked at Amma. She was frowning and rubbing her back.

The guard laughed. "Feel that? Those are tiny barbs sewn inside your jumpsuit. Only a prison guard knows where they are and what they look like, so we're the only ones who can move them with psi. Like I said, a little incentive."

Taemon let his mind wander inside the jumpsuit. Sure enough, he found dozens of little hooked disks between the jumpsuit's double layer of fabric. Aptly, the disks had a tiny Jaguar symbol engraved on them. Clever. Unless you knew about the Jaguar symbol, you couldn't envision the disks clearly enough to use psi on them. The plan just got a lot more painful.

The prisoners were led down a staircase at the end of the platform.

"Spread the new prisoners out," the head guard said. "Make sure each turbine gets three or four fresh grunts."

One of the guards pointed to Taemon, Amma, and Solovar. "You three come with me."

They stopped at the first cell. With psi, the guard opened the cell door and shoved Amma inside.

"Start turning, grunt," he said to Amma.

The prisoner who was being relieved emerged from the cell and left with the guard. His shoulders drooped, and he could barely keep his feet under him.

One by one, the guard exchanged each worn-out prisoner with a fresh one. Taemon found himself alone in his cell, watching the stripes on the turbine move past. He couldn't imagine working like this for hours and hours. It had to be the most boring, exhausting work ever.

He wouldn't be doing it, of course. Not without psi. He wouldn't be able to pull his share of the workload, which would make it harder for the others. He hoped they could get this done quickly.

If he couldn't turn the turbines, he could at least act as a lookout and alert the other prisoners if the guards were onto their plan. He looked up through the bars on the top of his cell. He saw the guards on the platform, watching the prisoners. But they had to look down to do that. None of them was looking up, where the screws were.

A sharp pain stung his back. One of those flaming hooks!

"You there!" one of the guards yelled. "Keep your eyes on the turbine."

He looked at the stripes sliding along and again wished he had psi. He had to rely on the others to ease the screws out silently. Hopefully they remembered what he'd told them in the hauler. One screw at a time. Unscrew it, float it across the ceiling, then hide it somewhere. He really hoped they'd all picked up on his clue about the elevator shaft! They were betting that the power plant might keep a few replacement screws on hand, but not enough to replace all of them at once. The guards would have to stop and hunt for the hidden screws. While the guards were looking for the screws and replacing them, the prisoners would try to escape.

When all of the guards were looking elsewhere, Taemon risked a glance at the top of the turbines. Yes, the screws were noiselessly coming out of position. *Careful,* he thought, *don't let them clang together.* He wished he could help somehow.

It was nerve-racking, trying to watch without looking up.

Three. Three of the five screws were out, and the fourth one was on its way. The stripes were slowing down. Almost there. He couldn't see the other turbines too well, but he hoped that the others were doing the same.

"Keep them turbines going, you dirty grunts!" screamed the head guard.

A flash of pain stung Taemon's back, but the barbs let up quickly.

Then he heard it: *Clink!*

Two of the screws had touched in midair.

The guards all looked up at the same time. "The screws!" one of them yelled.

Pain. Pain and noise is what happened next. Pain boring into his back in a dozen places. Taemon groaned. The other prisoners cried out, too. They lost their concentration, and the screws hovering in the air fell to the ground with a deafening noise. Noise and pain.

Taemon sank to his knees. He had failed. Again.

Once the clatter stopped, the head guard called out

orders to his subordinates. "Get them screws back in the turbines, men!"

The barbs stopped digging into Taemon's flesh, but the pain was still there. Now what? Skies, he couldn't even think anymore.

"What's going on?" the head guard bellowed. "Somebody's stealing them screws again. Who is it?"

More pain, but not as much this time. Taemon looked up. One by one, the screws were being floated across the room. As fast as the guards could get the screws from the floor back to the turbines, someone else was taking them out and dumping each one into the elevator shaft, just as they'd planned. But which of the prisoners was strong enough to do that? Everyone in Taemon's cell was doubled over with pain.

"Hoy, Taemon," a voice whispered. "I came to get you out of here."

Taemon turned around and saw someone crouched outside the cell door. "Moke?"

"Cha, it's me. Well, me and some of my friends. They're up there now, working on those screws."

"I don't understand," Taemon said. "I thought you were—"

"I didn't turn you in, I swear. It was my da. Someone squealed on me, told him what I was up to. He made a deal with the authorities. He told them where to find the rebels, and in exchange I went free."

"Thank the stars." Taemon felt huge relief knowing that Moke was still his friend. And that he cared enough to come to their rescue.

"We have to hurry," said Moke. "Can you use that clairvoyance thing to figure out this lock?"

Taemon turned his attention to the locks on the cell doors. He used his clairvoyance to examine the lock and uncover its design. They got lucky. It was something he could describe to Moke. "It's the Tramden clutch pattern, inverted stump, sixteen pins, pattern three-two-two-one-four," Taemon said. Moke's psi wasn't the strongest, but he could manage that much.

"Got it," Moke said. The lock released, and Taemon's cell door opened. "Are they all the same?"

Taemon quickly explored the other locks. "Cha."

Moke released the rest of the prisoners and waved them all over to a side door. The prisoner in the lead tried to open the door.

"I can't open it! It won't budge!"

"It's locked! We're trapped."

Panic was spreading through the group of prisoners. Taemon looked up to where the guards were running around, trying to find whoever was moving the screws.

"Hoy, Taemon!" It was Moke. "Tell us how to unlock this door. Hurry!"

It took all Taemon's concentration to calm himself enough to let his mind wander into the lock. Once he saw it, he called the pattern out to Moke and the door slid open.

Instantly, red and yellow lights began to flash. Sirens wailed.

"Prison break!" the head guard yelled above the din. "Get the serum!"

The sirens continued their blaring wails.

All the prisoners ran through the door except one. Solovar hadn't made it yet. Taemon searched the turbine room but didn't see him. He needed that man to help him get into the temple. He hoped Moke's friends were okay. He couldn't see them anywhere, either.

Suddenly Moke was at his side. "Come on, Taemon. Time to go!"

"But Solovar—"

"I'll make sure he gets out. Now go!"

Moke must have summoned all of the psi he possessed, because suddenly Taemon was pushed through the doorway. He turned back to wait for Moke.

"Down there! That kid without a jumpsuit. Get him!"

A length of metal pipe flew at Moke and pinned him against the wall by the throat. His feet dangled above the ground. He was choking.

"Moke!" Taemon cried. He ran to his friend's side, instantly feeling the hooks digging in again. He didn't care anymore. It hurt like flames, but it wouldn't kill him. Moke, on the other hand—he had to help Moke.

Taemon was desperately tugging on the metal pipe when he heard a voice booming from the platform. "Warden, order your men to stand down! We'll take it from here." Flames! It was Elder Naseph.

The pipe came free, and Taemon staggered back while Moke collapsed in a heap on the floor.

The barbs stopped gouging Taemon's back, but his flesh still felt the fire of their sting.

He knelt next to Moke and was surprised to find that Amma was right beside him. When had that happened?

"Hoy, Moke, it's Taemon."

Moke's eyelids fluttered. A nasty red mark on his neck was beginning to swell. His breathing sounded raspy and shallow. Skies! How badly was he hurt?

Taemon let his mind wander into Moke's body. Moke's breathing tube was crushed and torn in one spot. He explored deeper. Blood was flooding the breathing sacs instead of air. The injuries were bad, but they could save him if they hurried.

"Amma! Quick! His breathing tube. You need to fix it!"

Amma sat back on her heels. "You mean the trachea?"

"It's torn. Just a little psi would knit it together and push it back into shape. Then he can breathe again and cough up the blood."

Amma eyes became wide. "Taemon, I can't—"

"You've seen it in one of those books, haven't you? Just do it! Now!"

"I don't—I—"

"He's going to die!" Taemon yelled. "Do it!"

"I'll try." She stared intently at Moke.

Taemon sent his awareness back into Moke's injury. "Nothing's happening!"

Tears rolled down Amma's cheeks.

"Clear your head, Amma. Do it!"

"I can't," she whispered.

"Stop saying that! It's easy! Try again."

"I can't, Taemon!" She was yelling now. "I don't know what the tear looks like! I can't see it, and I can't do it! I'm sorry!"

A sob shook Taemon's shoulders. Knowledge without power. Power without knowledge. Neither Taemon nor Amma could help Moke.

Taemon used clairvoyance to look deeper into Moke's body, toward his heart. It wasn't beating. He was gone.

Gone.

Taemon dropped his chin to his chest.

Someone yanked him up from behind with psi. His arms were pulled behind his back. Cuffs closed over his wrists.

"The serum," a voice said. "For both of them."

Taemon felt a prick on the back of his neck. A strange sensation overtook him. First numbness, then dizziness. His clairvoyance seemed to come unbidden now and Taemon became aware of what was happening in his body.

He sensed the fluid they'd injected him with. He saw it coursing through his blood vessels, confusing his nerves and mixing up the messages to his brain. Did it even matter anymore?

"Moke," he whispered.

Then he blacked out.

19 FIRE

When Jaguar's finished, Fire ignites,
Giving off its warmth and light.
A Fire brings cheer to all around,
But it can burn things to the ground.
A Fire must be handled right.
A Fire must be handled right.

— CALENDAR SONG

Taemon woke up with a crick in his neck. His hands were still cuffed behind his back. He didn't move, but opened his eyes and stared at the burgundy-carpeted floor on which he lay. The place smelled musky, and he knew the scent. He'd been here only a few times before for family weddings and funerals, but that scent was unmistakable. He was inside the temple.

When he tried to sit up, even lifting his head off the floor made him woozy. He groaned.

He heard an unfamiliar voice somewhere in the room, but his head was spinning and he couldn't tell where the speaker was. "He's awake. Go get Elder Naseph."

Then he remembered everything. Moke was gone. A flood of grief washed over him. Was it over? Had they failed?

He wasn't eager to try lifting his head again, so he scanned the room moving only his eyes. It looked like an office of some kind. A desk. Chairs. Shelves on the walls with scrolls and boxes and baskets. He looked to his right. Amma lay on the floor next to him.

She was unconscious, but he could see that she was still breathing. Her nose had some blood on it, and her chin was scratched. Her face was relaxed and still; a few strands of hair fell across her cheek. He hadn't lost Amma. Yet.

He continued to stare at her. Once again he had the niggling feeling that he'd seen her somewhere before he had come to the colony.

And this time he remembered: he'd seen her in an image, a flash of vision when he'd almost killed Yens.

Yens looking down at the dead body of a pretty girl. Amma.

Yens pulling down the walls of a building. Amma's house.

Yens ordering armies into battle—that had been the third image. Skies above, Taemon could not let this happen. But how could he stop it?

As he watched her, Amma's eyelids flickered open. Her eyes were unfocused, and she moaned.

The door opened, and Taemon heard several people walk in.

Someone manhandled him into a sitting position. The humiliation of it barely registered as his head swam and he had to turn to the side and vomit. He hung his head until the spinning slowed, then looked up.

It was Yens. He sneered down at Taemon. "Is that any way to greet your long-lost brother?" He let go of Taemon's shoulders and turned to Amma. "Ah, I remember you."

"Leave her alone," said Taemon. He struggled to stand, but it was useless. He threw up again.

Yens shook Amma's shoulder. "Hello? Are we awake yet?"

Amma was unresponsive. Her eyes were closed. Taemon thought he'd seen her awake a minute ago, but either he'd been mistaken or she was out again.

"Leave her alone," Taemon repeated. "I'm the one you want."

Yens laughed. "Actually, it's you I *don't* want. But her, I might want."

"What are you going to do?" asked Taemon.

"The high priest has big plans for me, little brother. We're teaming up with the Republik to fight a war. After that, the psi wielders will take their place as true leaders of nations. Here's the best part: I get to lead the army. We've got psi weapons, and let me tell you, they are flaming incredible! Like nothing you've ever seen before. Those books we brought back from the colony—they had some powerful knowledge in them. Stuff not even the high priest knew existed! Now we can make more weapons, more powerful than before. When this war is over, Deliverance will take its rightful place in the world. There's no stopping the new Cycle of Power. And I'm the center of it."

Out of the corner of his eye, Taemon saw Amma stir. He needed to distract Yens, to keep Yens's focus on him and not Amma.

"Do you really think Elder Naseph gives a fig about

the True Son, Yens?" he asked, his words heavy with contempt. "You're just a figurehead to him. Someone he can use to excite the people of Deliverance and convince them that this war is a holy war."

Yens sniffed. "You've always been jealous of me. Admit it. When the high priest came to get me, a part of you wished he had come for you."

"Set aside your pride and think for a minute. The high priest is sending you to the Republik, right? Do you think he cares one squinch if you come back or not? Do you think anyone in the Republik cares? You're walking into a trap, Yens. A trap that gives Elder Naseph power over the Republik."

Yens's smirk faded just a little. Was Taemon actually getting through?

"You don't know that. How can you possibly know that?" Yens said.

"The woman that spoke to you in the colony—that was Challis. She's Mam's sister, the one that everyone thought had died. She can see the future, Yens. See what happens to you. You can't go to the Republik. You have to get away from the priests."

Yens took a step back. "Mam's dead sister sees the future? Listen to yourself, Taemon. That's nothing but klonk. The colonists have brainwashed you."

"It's not too late," Taemon pleaded. "You can do it. You can save your own life and countless others."

"I've heard enough," Yens said.

One of the temple guards stepped forward. "Should I give him another dose of the serum? Once they wake up, they need the second dose."

Taemon did feel a little stronger now that the room wasn't spinning and tilting so much.

"Don't waste any more serum on him. My brother's as powerless as a pebble."

"But Elder Naseph said—"

"I know what he said!" Yens yelled. "I'll take care of him. You're dismissed. All of you." He waved off all the temple guards, and they filed out of the room.

"What did Elder Naseph say?" Taemon asked.

Yens spat on the floor. "Naseph doesn't know what he's talking about. He thinks that he has a weird kind of psi called precognition. Klonkiest thing I've ever heard. He claims he had a vision of you getting your psi back and frustrating our plan somehow." Yens snorted. "The crazy old goat would only agree to leave me alone with you if I promised to get rid of you for good."

Despite Yens's dire warning, a tiny spark of hope flashed in Taemon's mind. If Elder Naseph had seen him getting his psi back, then somehow it had to be possible. He could stop this terrible war. He could put things right. But how? How could he get his psi back?

Ask and you shall receive.

Holy Skies above! The voice was back!

Yens paced the room. "Did you know there are seventeen ways to instantly kill a person with psi? The priests have taught me all of them. We practiced. First on cadavers, then on the innocents. It was amazing."

Taemon fought to keep the horror from showing on his face. He needed to stop Yens. He needed his psi back. But the voice still troubled him. It couldn't be Challis. It didn't sound like her at all. But what was it? Was it evil? Was it good? Was it insanity? He had to know.

Ask and it shall be answered.

Yens continued his rant. "And speaking of prisoners, did you know that Mam and Da were taken to the asylum? Mam lost her wits when you were taken away, and Da started speaking up during church services. They were menaces to society, both of them."

Anxiety clogged Taemon's thoughts, but he pushed it away. This information only increased the need to get his psi back. And that meant he had to focus.

Who are you? Taemon asked the voice.

I am the Heart of the Earth. The spirit of the planet. The consciousness that connects all living things.

Taemon was awestruck. Either he had a direct connection with the deity of his fathers or he was going loopy. Right now, he had to believe it was the former.

Which meant he could get his psi back. The idea flared and leaped like a fire in his mind.

Consider carefully. You cannot request a gift only to discard it at will. If you ask me to restore your power, the restoration will be permanent.

Yens paced back and forth, rubbing his chin. "So what will it be? Stop the heart? Sever the brain stem?" He stopped. "I know." A slow smile curled his lips. "Suffocation. As I recall, you were rather fond of that one."

Before Yens could blink, a chair flew across the room, tripping Yens and then pinning him down.

Taemon looked at Amma. She was fully awake now, sitting up and glaring at Yens.

Yens laughed. "Oh, good. This will be more fun. I won't even give you another dose of the serum. Very sporting of me, don't you think?" He heaved the chair upward with psi, smashing it against the wall. He stood up.

Amma's neck and arms looked strained, as if she was trying to move but couldn't. Yens must be keeping her in place with his psi.

"Now I understand why you didn't want people to know about your brother," Amma said to Taemon. "He's a monster."

Yens yanked Taemon and Amma up. Taemon felt his throat constricting. He was dangling, his toes only barely touching the floor. If he had to die, thought Taemon, at least he would die the same way Moke did.

But only if he had to. It was time to ask. *Can you give me psi?* thought Taemon.

You have been prepared for this task. You must act with great care, for your choices will determine the nature of the next Great Cycle. *You* **are the True Son.**

Yens looked at Taemon. "I could kill the girl. Then you

could watch her die. Or maybe she should watch you die."
Yens lifted Amma a few inches, then Taemon, as though literally weighing his options.

I will. Please! Give me psi!

Be it so.

20 FRUIT

Fire dies and Fruit is born.

The tree yields plum; the stalk grows corn.

Just as Fruit begins as seed,

Results are sown with every deed.

When harvest comes, rejoice or mourn.

When harvest comes, rejoice or mourn.

— CALENDAR SONG

A tremendous power came to him immediately, waiting to be directed. Taemon used it to push Yens against the wall and hold him there.

"What?" Yens shouted. The break in Yens's concentration allowed Taemon and Amma to breathe deeply. Next, Taemon mind-wandered into the lock on the psi cuffs, sensed how it worked, and unlocked both his and Amma's restraints at the same time. It was all done in an instant.

Taemon could sense Yens's psi opposing his own. He had to use every bit of concentration to keep Yens pinned against the wall.

Amma stared at him, her eyes wide and her mouth open. "How . . . ?"

"Find the serum," Taemon told Amma.

She snapped out of her daze and searched the room, rifling through the drawers, searching the shelves, even upending a fruit basket. "I can't find anything that looks right!"

A plum rolled across the floor and knocked against Taemon's foot. "Keep looking." He used psi to pull Yens's hands into a pair of cuffs. But cuffs didn't do anything to impair psi. They needed the serum for that.

He tried to find the serum with mind wandering, but it didn't seem to be in the room anywhere, and wandering any farther out would weaken his ability to keep Yens subdued.

Yens tugged harder with psi. Taemon knew he couldn't keep this up forever.

There was one thing he could try. He sent his mind wandering into Yens's body. He recalled what the serum had done to him—sent the wrong messages to the brain, confused the nerves—and he worked to do the same things inside Yens's body.

Yens's eyes glazed over, and his chin dropped to his chest.

He couldn't believe that it had worked! Taemon wiped the sweat from his face.

Amma looked at Yens, collapsed on the floor. "Did you kill him?" she whispered.

"No!" Taemon said. "Do you really think I would do that? He's unconscious, but I don't know for how long."

"We should lock the door," Amma said.

"No, they'll know how to unlock it."

"Then we run? Go back to the colony?" Amma looked to him for an answer, but he had none.

"I'm afraid it's too late for that." Elder Naseph stood in the doorway, calmly surveying the scene. "I knew this moment would come. I saw it. The power outage you masterminded was quite impressive. Rather poetic. A powerless person creating a power outage." Elder Naseph chuckled and strolled into the room with all his fine airs and tinkling noises.

"Nothing about this is funny or poetic," Taemon said. "It's downright evil."

The priest looked disappointed. "Now, now, we have much to talk about. Shall we call a truce and discuss our options? Absolutely no psi, you have my word." He held out his hands, palms upward.

Amma scoffed. "Your word? Do you think we trust your word?"

"I'm not worried about your psi," Taemon said. "And I'm not interested in what you have to say. You and the other priests need to put a stop to this war. I won't let you send Yens to the Republik."

Elder Naseph chuckled. "Stop the war? Dear Brother Houser. It is not my war to stop."

"What do you mean?" Amma asked.

"The war is already going on all around us. Deliverance has been an oasis of peace. But it can't last. The Republik needs our help. We cannot sit idly by and watch our neighbor nation torn apart by war. The era of isolation is past. As for your brother, who better to wield our unstoppable weapons? He'll have to live with the Republikites, that's true, but think of him as an ambassador."

Amma snorted. "Sounds more like a hostage."

Taemon's mind was reeling. "So . . . the war . . . Everything is . . ." The sentences were too horrific to complete. "If your plans are in place, why do you need the library?"

Elder Naseph smiled. "I thought you had no interest in hearing what I have to say."

"Just get on with it," Taemon ordered.

"Very well. I want you to understand, young Taemon, because you have played an important role in all this. The Republik is a strong nation. Psiless, mind you, but well organized. Highly militarized. Making an alliance with them is nothing to play at. They have a history of turning on their allies. But when we decided to end the long isolation of Deliverance and take our place in world leadership, we knew we'd need the Republik on our side, at least to begin with. They wanted psi weapons and someone who could use them. We could provide that. But we needed something more, some coveted treasure that we could hold against them to keep them in their place. The library is perfect. It seems they've lost some of that knowledge themselves and would do just about anything to get it back."

"The library is not a bargaining chip!" Amma said. "It belongs to the colony."

"It belongs to the people," Elder Naseph said. "We're

just taking it back. Not only can we create more powerful weapons for ourselves, but as long as we have the books in our hands, we can make sure the Republik doesn't double-cross us and try to use our own weapons against us. So you see? This way, everyone gets what they want."

"No one wants war," Taemon said.

"Oh, I disagree with that." Elder Naseph tsked. "Plenty of people want war." He smiled and folded his arms in front of his chest. "So I really must thank you for bringing us the library. The way you discerned the psi lock was most impressive. Oh, yes, we knew it was you," Elder Naseph said when Taemon stiffened in shock. "Your brother proved useful for a time, but we quickly discovered that he was not as gifted as we'd been led to believe.

"But you, young Taemon. You have gifts you may not even be aware you possess. I can help you uncover those gifts, master them. We can work together, you and I. In the New Cycle, I plan to appoint new priests. Younger priests. How would you like that, Elder Taemon?" He chuckled. "Wouldn't your da be proud."

"Absolutely not," Taemon said.

"Perhaps you'd rather be the True Son." Elder Naseph jangled the trinkets in his beard. "That could be arranged."

His calculating tone was sickening. Taemon *was* the True Son, and Elder Naseph had nothing to do with it. Da had been right to view the priests' presumptuousness with contempt.

"I'll never lead your army," said Taemon. "I'll never use psi to hurt people."

The priest waved his hand dismissively. "We won't be hurting anyone. I expect one demonstration will be sufficient for the world to surrender to our leadership. We could get rid of Mount Deliverance. Pull down the mountains that separate us from the Republik as a sign of goodwill. Then we can join forces with the Republik and help them win the war. After that . . . just think for a moment. Who do you think will lead the Republik after the war? Why, the psi wielders, of course. Namely you and I, the most powerful of psi wielders."

"You think we believe that?" Amma interrupted. "You're just trying to get Taemon on your side, where you can keep him under your thumb."

Taemon weighed his options. What could he do to stop Naseph? He already had the library, Yens's cooperation, and the treaty with the Republik, none of which Taemon had the power to take away, even with psi. Maybe he should give in for now and agree to work with Naseph. Later he could find another way to defeat the high priest's plan. He had to admit, having psi again felt wonderful. And he still had clairvoyance as well. There would be almost nothing he couldn't do.

But Challis had been so sure that this was his one chance to stop the war. Could she have been wrong? Would there be another chance somewhere down the road?

If he could only figure out what exactly he should do.

Choose wisely, for this choice has great consequences. This choice determines the nature of the next Great Cycle. You have been chosen to make this decision on behalf of all.

Could he really work with the priests? Try to turn them around? They had powerful psi. They'd gotten their hands on dangerous knowledge. It was a disastrous combination, no matter what side Taemon chose.

There are yet many paths, many choices.

What other choices? Taemon had never felt like he had so few choices in his life.

Something that Amma had said came into his mind. What you want determines who you are. The real problem here was the high priest's greedy, hateful ways. If he could get rid of that, he could solve everything.

Is there a way to change a person's heart? Take the evil desires away?

Free will is gift that even I cannot take away.

So he couldn't force anyone to be virtuous. But what if he were the leader? What if Taemon Houser were telling people what to do? Could he stop rewarding greed and pride and motivate people to help one another?

It is possible. Think carefully. Choose wisely.

Three temple guards entered the room. "Elder Naseph, there's trouble outside the temple," the head guard said.

"Trouble?" Elder Naseph kept his eyes on Taemon, but his words were meant for the guards. "What kind of trouble?"

"A crowd," said the guard. "An . . . unruly crowd. They're chanting something. We don't know what."

Elder Naseph used psi to open a set of ornately etched glass doors, which led out to some kind of balcony. With the doors open, the chanting became clear.

"Young Moke! Young Moke! Young Moke!"

"Ah, yes," said Naseph. "The unfortunate accident at the power plant. This will work perfectly into our plans, Taemon. The people are ready for change, hungry for something more. The time has come to reshape our society."

Anger swelled in Taemon's chest. Moke's death worked perfectly into their plans? Not for Moke it didn't. And not for Taemon.

"Young Moke! Young Moke!" The chanting became louder.

"Your moment has come, Taemon. Step out on the balcony with me, and I will introduce you as the new True Son."

Without waiting to see if Taemon would follow, the old priest walked out onto the balcony. He motioned for quiet.

Amma put her hand on Taemon's arm. There was more power in that touch than in all the psi coursing through their bodies. "Picture what you want," she whispered. "Then make it happen. Just be sure of what you want."

"My brothers and sisters," Elder Naseph called out to the crowd. "We knew that the beginning of the Great Cycle would bring many astonishing events, and today has brought much astonishment. Darkness in our city. An unfortunate loss of a young man. Young Moke died because he was brave enough to stand up for his friends and for the important changes that must take place. Let us memorialize young Moke's death by enacting these changes."

The crowd's chanting turned into applause.

"Now I wish to make known to you another astonishing event. The True Son has proven himself unworthy. He has confessed to lying about his own abilities, his greed and ambition having blinded him to what was right. But fear not! Another True Son shall take his place."

The crowd murmured its confusion.

"This young man is a True Son worthy of the name and of the honor! He is uniquely qualified to act as an ambassador between the powerless world and our own, for he himself was once powerless, but now he is the most powerful among us, the one who will lead us into a Great Cycle of prosperity! Taemon Houser, the new True Son."

The crowd was silent. Elder Naseph had tried to make it a momentous occasion, but even Taemon felt it was clumsy and false. Taemon stepped forward to the edge of the balcony and looked down at the crowd. He saw Solovar standing in front. Taemon knew the crowd was waiting for him to speak, but he had no idea what to say. He opened his mouth and hoped something intelligent would come out.

Before Taemon could say a word, the balcony began to shake. Just a tremble at first, then enough to make him stumble and grab the railing. What in the Great Green Earth? He turned around and saw Yens standing in the doorway.

"I am the True Son," Yens said. "I am the True Son!"

The temple shook again.

Amma gasped. "An earthquake."

Taemon knew he had to do something. He tried to connect with Yens's body and confuse his brain signals, as he'd done before. But it wasn't working. Yens's heart was beating fast, and his brain was in some kind of super-excited state.

The carved railings of the temple balcony broke off and fell to the ground below. Taemon took a few staggering steps away from the edge.

He sent his awareness into the earth underneath him, trying to figure out what Yens was doing to cause the earthquake. He could tell that Yens had shifted something out of balance, but Taemon hadn't seen what the earth had looked like before Yens had shifted it. Taemon couldn't be sure how to put it back without causing more damage.

The earthquake was getting worse. The floor of the balcony cracked, and chunks of the walls broke loose.

Yens's eyes were wild. His hands were clenched into fists. The cords on his neck stood out. "You. Are *not*. The True Son." His words came between panting breaths.

I have to end this, thought Taemon. *I have to end this right now.*

You are permitted to end his life.

No, Taemon answered the voice in his mind. *I already made that decision. I will not kill my own brother.*

Images flashed in his mind. Mam screaming in agony. He and Amma running for their lives from something big and dark that chased them. An explosion in the city.

Choose wisely.

He wouldn't kill Yens, but he had to find another way to stop his brother.

Moke's death flashed in Taemon's mind. He tried to shove his sadness away until he realized that it was part of the solution. Moke died because Taemon's knowledge was useless without power and Amma's power was useless without knowledge. If he could separate Yens's knowledge from the power . . .

It reminded him of what Challis had said: "When virtue is missing, power must be separated from knowledge." Skies, he must be going klonky if Challis's words were starting to make sense. But klonky or not, he had to do something. Now.

The floor of the balcony snapped, then tilted. The temple walls groaned and cracked. Taemon used clairvoyance to examine its foundations and found they were badly damaged. The temple could collapse any second. He could probably fix it, but somehow it seemed right to let the temple fall. The greed of the priests had brought the downfall of their society.

He turned to Amma. "You have to get out of here."

"I'm not leaving without you," she said.

Taemon looked over the precarious edge of the balcony. "Use psi to stack some of that rubble into something we can climb down on," Taemon said.

Amma nodded.

Now to deal with Yens. Was it possible to take away Yens's psi? After all, he'd done it to himself not more than a year ago.

Think carefully. Choose wisely.

Finally! A solution that might work! He could take psi away from Yens and maybe from the priests, too. And from anyone else who had a mind to do evil. But he'd need a way to distinguish the good people from the bad ones. How would he do that? And did he really have the right to decide who could have psi and who couldn't? That sounded awfully like something the priests would do.

An idea was shaping itself in Taemon's mind. At first he pushed it aside. It was unthinkable. Foolish. Insane. But the thought wouldn't leave. It did solve the problem, after all.

Think carefully.

But it would cause so many new problems.

The temple shuddered, as if in its death spasms.

Choose wisely.

New problems that could also be solved.

The floor under Taemon's feet dropped another foot or two.

You must choose. On behalf of your people, you must choose.

Taemon gathered his psi and focused his thoughts.

Let all psi in Deliverance be done away with! Taemon

cried to the Heart of the Earth. *Let each man and woman work by the power of their own hands. Let this begin the Great Cycle!*

Be it so.

The words echoed through his mind, his heart, his bones, his flesh.

21 ALLIGATOR

Each new cycle must begin
With Alligator creeping in.
Unseen danger now surrounds you.
New awareness must be found to
Conquer fear from deep within.
Conquer fear from deep within.

— CALENDAR SONG

The earthquake stopped abruptly.

"What did you do?" Yens yelled. With one last horrified look at Taemon, Yens ran back inside the temple.

"It's going to collapse!" Taemon started to run after Yens, but Amma held him back.

"Let Yens make his choice," she said.

The floor lurched beneath Taemon's feet. Even though the earthquake had stopped, the balcony was teetering on an unstable foundation.

Taemon stared at the door Yens had just disappeared through. Where were the priests? Had they gone inside, too?

"We have to go!" Amma said. "Now!"

Taemon and Amma hurried down the rubble. Just as they reached the ground, the temple wobbled one last time, then fell into a heap of stone and wood and dust.

When the upheaval ended, everything felt eerily tranquil.

"Was that you?" Amma asked. "Did you do that?"

"No. I did something else. Something people are not going to like."

"Whatever it was, if it stops the war, it will be worth it."

Taemon hoped she was right.

The people who had gathered at the temple had backed away and watched the temple fall. Taemon and Amma went to join them.

Solovar stepped forward. "What happened? Where are the priests?"

Amma spoke up. "The last time I saw them, they were running into the temple."

"They were inside?" Solovar asked.

"I think so," Amma whispered. "Yens, too."

"Let's clear away this rubble, people," Solovar said.

That's when the real panic started.

"I can't do anything!"

"What's wrong with me?"

"Where is my psi?"

"Is yours gone, too?"

"Skies! Does anyone still have psi?"

"The temple! It must have happened when the temple fell down."

The voices grew louder and more anxious. He knew how they felt. Learning how to be powerless would be hard, very hard. But when he thought about the alternative—war, destruction, suffering—he knew he'd made the right choice.

He watched Amma's face as she began to piece together what had happened. Her eyes slowly widened. "I think it's better if we go back to the colony for now," she whispered. "If they find out it was you, you'll be in real danger. We'll send back some people who can help."

"Wait," said Solovar. "Let me go with you."

Without thinking, Taemon put a hand on Solovar's shoulder. But Solovar didn't even flinch. "The people here need you, Solovar. You can help them rebuild Deliverance.

The colonists will teach you how to build things that don't require psi to operate, how to plant and harvest food. Life can be good again."

Solovar rubbed his hand over the white stubble on his chin. His fingers left streaks in the dust covering his face. He took a deep breath. "Skies above. It really is a new cycle."

Amma and Taemon took advantage of all the confusion to slip out of the temple grounds, down the steps, and out to the street.

The traffic lights had stopped working, but it didn't matter because the quadriders had stopped running as well, their drivers puzzled. Some had gotten out of their vehicles and were banging on the hoods, unsure how to open them without psi. One woman was sitting on the curb, holding her head in her hands and rocking her body. Children were crying, and their parents were holding them awkwardly.

"So it's gone?" Amma asked. "Psi is really gone?"

Taemon nodded. "It was the only way."

"Your parents would be proud," Amma said. "It was the right thing."

"But not the easy thing."

At a restaurant, people were climbing out of broken windows because no one could get the automatic doors to work. Some people ran; others wandered in a stupor.

"This is going to get worse before it gets better," Amma whispered.

"It will take a long time to get used to," Taemon said. "But they'll adapt."

"Let's go home," Amma said. "Which way?"

"This way," said Taemon, pointing to the Alligator street sign. "It's the quickest."

He took her hand. Amid the pandemonium, Taemon and Amma walked calmly through the streets and left Deliverance through the North Gate.

ACKNOWLEDGMENTS

Writing is often considered a solitary endeavor, but really it's a team sport. I am lucky to belong to an amazing team helping me at every point in the game.

My miracle-worker agent, Molly Jaffa, saw something thoroughly cool in Taemon despite the clumsiness of my early efforts. Kaylan Adair brought her editing prowess to bear on *Freakling*. My writing group comrades have lent their unfailing support over the years. Brian Rock, Stephanie McPherson, Hazel Buys, and Pat Tabb from the Richmond Children's Writers and Neysa Jensen, Docena Holm, Monelle Smith, Michelle Tripp, Brenda Cordery, Zenija Blatz, Jo Mitchell, and Laura Bingham from the Treasure Valley Children's Writers have all had a hand in Taemon's story. Beta readers Kristen Fennel and Katelyn Chrisman were a big help. Also vital to the effort was in-house reader Ben Krumwiede.

I feel sorry for anyone who has a writer in their immediate family. Writers are always pestering the nearest innocent bystander (usually family members) by throwing story ideas around and insisting on brainstorming sessions. My family has cheerfully endured a great deal of mind wandering and story obsessing.

Many thanks all around!